Acting Edition

I0741574

The Ally

by Itamar Moses

FOR PRODUCTION INQUIRIES

UNITED STATES AND CANADA
info@concordtheatricals.com
1-866-979-0447

UNITED KINGDOM AND EUROPE
licensing@concordtheatricals.co.uk
020-7054-7298

Each title is subject to availability from Concord Theatricals Corp., depending upon country of performance. Please be aware that *THE ALLY* may not be licensed by Concord Theatricals Corp. in your territory. Professional and amateur producers should contact the nearest Concord Theatricals Corp. office or licensing partner to verify availability.

No one shall make any changes in this title(s) for the purpose of production. No part of this book may be reproduced, stored in a retrieval system, scanned, uploaded, or transmitted in any form, by any means, now known or yet to be invented, including mechanical, electronic, digital, photocopying, recording, videotaping, or otherwise, without the prior written permission of the publisher. No one shall share this title(s), or any part of this title(s), through any social media or file hosting websites.

For all inquiries regarding motion picture, television, online/digital and other media rights, please contact Concord Theatricals Corp.

MUSIC AND THIRD-PARTY MATERIALS USE NOTE

Licensees are solely responsible for obtaining formal written permission from copyright owners to use copyrighted music and/or other copyrighted third-party materials (e.g. artworks, logos) in the performance of this play and are strongly cautioned to do so. If no such permission is obtained by the licensee, then the licensee must use only original music and materials that the licensee owns and controls. Licensees are solely responsible and liable for clearances of all third-party copyrighted materials, including without limitation music, and shall indemnify the copyright owners of the play(s) and their licensing agent, Concord Theatricals Corp., against any costs, expenses, losses and liabilities arising from the use of such copyrighted third-party materials by licensees. For music, please contact the appropriate music licensing authority in your territory for the rights to any incidental music.

IMPORTANT BILLING AND CREDIT REQUIREMENTS

If you have obtained performance rights to this title, please refer to your licensing agreement for important billing and credit requirements.

THE ALLY was first produced by the Public Theater (Oskar Eustis, Artistic Director; Patrick Willingham, Executive Director) in New York and opened on February 15, 2024. The production was directed by Lila Neugebauer, with scenic design by Lael Jellinek, costume design by Sarita Fellows, lighting design by Reza Behjat, and sound design by Bray Poor. The production stage manager was Roxana Khan. The cast was as follows:

ASAF STERNHEIM	Josh Radnor
GWEN KIM	Joy Osmanski
BARON PRINCE	Elijah Jones
NAKIA CLARK/RABBI	Cherise Boothe
RACHEL KLEIN	Madeline Weinstein
FARID EL MASRY	Michael Khalid Karadsheh
REUVEN FISHER	Ben Rosenfield

CHARACTERS

ASAF STERNHEIM – 40s, Jewish, a writer, and an adjunct professor of writing

GWEN KIM – late 30s, Korean American, University Administrator for Community Relations and External Affairs, Asaf's wife

BARON PRINCE – 21, African American, a college senior

NAKIA CLARK – 40s, African American, a community organizer (doubles with **THE RABBI**)

RACHEL KLEIN – 20, Jewish, a college junior

FARID EL MASRY – 20, Palestinian American, a college junior

REUVEN FISHER – 29, Jewish, a PhD student in Jewish History and Judaic Studies

SETTING

A prestigious American university in a struggling American city somewhere in New England or maybe farther down the East Coast or possibly in the Midwest.

TIME

September 2023.

AUTHOR'S NOTE

The Ally works best when every single character is portrayed as making their arguments in good faith. Resist any temptation to put a finger on the scale by telegraphing one or another character's "wrongness" or "badness" – this is to oversimplify, as well as to deny the audience the opportunity to experience the play completely and honestly.

ACT ONE

(**ASAF** *and* **GWEN**.)

GWEN. Oh, hey: have you thought any more about the holidays?

ASAF. Oh! Um –

GWEN. Yeah cuz when I brought up doing it just us, here, you seemed *kinda* into that? But then sorta...never decided? So –

ASAF. Right.

GWEN. But if you *did* still want to go to California, to see family, we'd need to start thinking about tickets and hotels, like, *soon*.

ASAF. Right, no, I mean... On the one hand, when you suggested that it sounded potentially really nice?

GWEN. Right? Cozy, quiet –

ASAF. Yeah.

GWEN. – Not responsible for defusing tension amongst the lunatic personalities around us.

ASAF. Right. *(Then –)* There should actually be a dating app for helping the not-crazy members of each family find each other.

GWEN. *(She thinks. Then –)* "Saner."

ASAF. Write that down.

GWEN. But, okay, so is that –

ASAF. Well, so the only thing... First of all, I'm a little nervous breaking the news?

GWEN. Oh.

ASAF. Yeah, you know how they get: under the thin surface of Israeli-immigrant stoicism is plain old Jewish guilt. Plus: there are things I really love about going home, so –

GWEN. Okay, well: you know which *I'd* prefer, but, whatever you decide, lemme know with enough time to plan. I know the semester just started but, before you know it, October'll sneak up and then –

ASAF. Yeah, will do. *(This reminds him –)* Oh! How'd the meeting go?

GWEN. Oh, yeah, good.

ASAF. Good! You were nervous.

GWEN. Well the University doesn't have the best history around expansion.

ASAF. Right.

GWEN. Yeah. So we knew there was gonna be resistance. But I think we did a good job explaining how it could be...mutually beneficial this time.

ASAF. Right. How?

GWEN. Oh, you know, for every unit of student housing we commit to building one of *affordable*. And every student who *lives* there has to volunteer, tutoring or... guiding promising local kids through admissions. We protect local *business* instead of... Y'know.

ASAF. Right. Great!

GWEN. Yeah. I mean there's a lot of boards and votes to get through? But: so far so good! *(Then –)* How 'bout you? How was writing today?

ASAF. Pretty *good*, actually.

GWEN. *(Pleasantly surprised –)* Oh! *That's* nice.

ASAF. Yeah, I've been stuck, I know, but I sorta had a breakthrough.

GWEN. This is nineteenth-century Germany.

ASAF. Von Bismark, yeah. "His chess-like diplomacy unified the country and his marriage. But he abused underlings and was secretly in love with a dead woman his whole life. So does stability just mean you've directed your insanity elsewhere?"

GWEN. Uh-oh. Does it?

ASAF. I will let you know. *(Then –)* But, yeah, another play about **Enlightenment** Europe. Don't know why I keep doing that.

GWEN. Yeah, I don't know either.

(Pause.)

ASAF. Hey if we *did* do the holidays here, just us, would that be *just* us? Which, I'm not saying... That would be nice! I'm just asking cuz *I* don't really – I mean *you* know people at the **university** but *I* don't really know them so... I'm just asking.

GWEN. Right, no. I'm not sure. What do you think?

ASAF. Yeah, I'll...think about it.

GWEN. Okay. *(A moment. Then –)* Hey, listen. You've been incredibly supportive. But if you ever have second thoughts about us having moved here?

ASAF. Whoa, what?

GWEN. No, I'm just saying: I know we talked about it when I first got the offer but that doesn't mean we can't ever revisit this decision. If you're unhappy, and you wanna try, I don't know, splitting time, or –

ASAF. I don't.

GWEN. Okay but you can *tell* me.

ASAF. When this job came up, *I* said, "That's perfect. You *have* to go for that."

GWEN. Yeah but I'm asking about *you*.

ASAF. Well and this has been good for me too! *(Off her –)* Really! It's a nice neighborhood. There's…*space. (Beat.)* If we decide to have a *kid*, they get a break on *tuition* in eighteen years.

GWEN. This is not making me feel better.

ASAF. Are you sure? Cuz that's a good perk. *(Off her –)* Okay, no, look: New York was great. I love New York. But it obviously hasn't been the *same* these last few years. And I can do *my* work anywhere…theoretically. *(Beat.)* Plus, I *love* college towns. I grew *up* in a college town. I went to *college* in a college town. It's kinda like coming home.

GWEN. Okay! *(Beat.)* But then can I make a suggestion without you getting mad?

ASAF. Let's find out.

GWEN. No, just… I wonder if maybe you should try to get more…involved. *Locally*, like: join an *activity* or some –

ASAF. What, like take a spin class or join a book club?

GWEN. Well it would be nice if it were something for which you were not preemptively dripping with *contempt* but –

ASAF. Why?

GWEN. *Why?* Cuz you don't have anything to *do* other than try to write all day 'til I get home and it's making you *miserable*.

ASAF. I *just said* it went well!

GWEN. Yeah, *today*. Which is why I'm saying this *now*: you're less likely to bite my head off. But we *both know*, as soon as that *stops*, you'll be back in a funk. So, *before* that, maybe figure out a few other...sources of stimuli that could balance your life. I mean we *do* get discounts at everything affiliated with the school: museums, concerts. You could go to the campus synagogue!

ASAF. What?

GWEN. I hear the Rabbi's cool.

ASAF. I'm an *atheist*.

GWEN. Not to *pray*! To...! They have *events*, speakers –!

ASAF. And I *do* have an activity. I teach.

GWEN. *One* class.

ASAF. I teach playwriting, screenwriting and TV writing.

GWEN. That's *one class*. You teach *one* day a week, *one* semester a year. You literally teach *fourteen days* a *year*. No, look: I'm not saying you don't work hard. Just the opposite. You're working *constantly*, in your *head*. Right now you're like someone who's exhaling non-stop and wonders why he's out of *breath*. *I'm* just saying breathe *in* once in a while. In *fact*: don't you *have* a friend here? *(Then, off him –)* Your ex. From college.

ASAF. Oh. *(Beat.)* Well, yeah, she...grew *up* here and then moved *back* I think. But she's not a friend, she's an ex.

GWEN. Okay. So? *(Then, off him –)* I mean, don't not call her on *my* account. *I* don't care who you were sleeping with when you were twenty-*three*, or –

ASAF. No, no, nothing like that, it's just... We haven't really kept in touch. I mean it's been, like, yeah, twenty years. More.

GWEN. Fine. *Don't* call her. The point is: maybe get out of the *house*.

ASAF. I am, I will. In fact, I'm getting out of the house *tomorrow*.

GWEN. *(Pleased –)* Oh! For what?

ASAF. Office hours.

GWEN. *(Less pleased –)* Oh.

ASAF. Yeah, a student from last semester wants to meet. Baron Prince? *(Off her blank look –)* He sorta wrote the...best script in class. Two-thirds of it, anyway. He didn't quite finish.

GWEN. What about?

ASAF. The...presumably autobiographical story of a black kid from a rough neighborhood that *abuts* a prestigious university, which he then ends up *attending*, forcing him to sort of *straddle* –

GWEN. *(That wasn't her question –)* What does he wanna *meet* about.

ASAF. *Oh.* Not sure. But he's a *senior* now? So probably how to break into the industry or get an agent or something. That's usually what they want to meet about at this stage.

GWEN. Is that annoying?

ASAF. When they're bad *writers*, yeah. But, like I said, he's good. So it's fine. I'm actually looking forward to seeing him.

        (**ASAF** *and* **BARON**.)

BARON. Good to see you too.

ASAF. How was your summer? You finish that script?

BARON. What? Naw. I mean, I *tried*, but –

ASAF. Oh you gotta! That thing was really good.

BARON. Thanks. It was just...kinda hard to focus with everything, so –

ASAF. What? What do you mean?

BARON. You serious?

ASAF. No, did...something happen? We were away most of the summer and when I'm here I don't get out much or...talk to anyone, so –

BARON. You didn't hear about Deronte Lee.

ASAF. Oh. Wait, yes. Police brutality, right?

BARON. Well they...killed him, so –

ASAF. Yeah, no, I *did*. Wait, did you *know* him?

BARON. He was my cousin.

ASAF. Oh god. *(Beat.)* Oh god, I'm *so sorry*.

BARON. Thanks. Yeah, it's been a lot.

ASAF. I bet. Jesus. How *are* you? Are you...okay, or –?

BARON. I mean, it's worse for my aunt. His kid sister. So just...trying to be there for them, which...gives me something to *do*.

ASAF. Right. Were you close?

BARON. I mean...more when we were little? Not so much lately. But still –

ASAF. Right, no.

BARON. Did you see the video?

ASAF. No. I mean: I saw there *was* one? But just out of *respect*... I mean, a video where someone *dies*?

BARON. You should watch it.

ASAF. Oh! Okay. I mean, yeah, I will. Yes. *(Beat.)* Yeah, *sorry*: this is *your* time.

BARON. What?

ASAF. No, just: we can talk about this for as long as *you* want. Obviously. I just want to make sure we *also* meet about whatever you wanted to *meet* about.

BARON. This *is* what I want to meet about.

ASAF. Oh. *(Beat.)* Sorry, so –

BARON. Yeah lemme back up.

ASAF. Okay.

BARON. Cuz, first of all – and, again, you should just watch the video, cuz I can explain it? But it's sorta undeniable once you –

ASAF. No, I'm sure.

BARON. But just so you know what happened, cuz you said you don't talk to anyone.

ASAF. Well –

BARON. But, basically, someone had been stealing cars from *campus* lots, which: can't have *that*, right? So the cops are extra on guard, extra vigilant, and then one day someone calls in someone "acting suspicious" around a campus parking lot and so, like, *eight* cops head down there right away. And Deronte happens to be in the neighborhood, cuz he, you know, *lives* in the *neighbor*hood, so he's just walking by, and... And I don't know if he's even the person that, um, Parking Lot Karen saw? But he musta, um, "matched the description," plus one of the cops apparently recognized him from...whatever: whatever petty bullshit he'd done in the past, graffiti, or having an ounce of weed, *nothing* serious, *definitely* not stealing *cars*. But so dude's like: "Hey you. Stop." And Deronte's like, "Why? What did I do?" But *that's* resisting, right? "Contempt of cop"? So they just slam him to the ground and... *(Pause.)* **This is the other reason you should just watch, cuz I don't really wanna –**

ASAF. No, of course. –

BARON. In their, like, initial statement? They said he grabbed for their guns and so they "feared for their lives." But in the video, you can see he didn't. He just keeps asking, "What did I do? What did I do?" *(Beat.)* Then like a hour later they caught the guy, the *real* guy, who'd been stealing cars, *in* one of the cars that he stole.

ASAF. Un-fucking-believable.

BARON. Yeah.

> *(Beat.)*

ASAF. And so... What, you wanna...find a way to *write* about it? Or –

BARON. What? *No.*

ASAF. Oh, okay.

BARON. Yeah, no, it made me wanna actually *do* something.

ASAF. Oh. *(Beat.)* No, right –

BARON. Yeah, so, I joined this group. This, like, activist group? Voice to Action? Run by this local organizer lady who's been agitating about this stuff for a while. Actually, Nakia contacted *me* cuz –

ASAF. Wait, Nakia *Clark*?

BARON. Oh, you know her?

ASAF. I know...*a* Nakia Clark. Who *lives* here and I think does this kind of *work*.

BARON. Well that's probably her then. Anyway, yeah, so she got the family involved, and, cuz I'm *at* the university, that's part of it too, cuz this is part of a loooooong history of –

ASAF. No, sure.

BARON. – Yeah, how this town works, which is like two different towns.

ASAF. Right.

BARON. Yeah, *you* know. Anyway so: we have *this*...

> *(He pulls a document out of his bag.)*

...I guess you could call it..."manifesto"? Modelled on some other ones about reforms that can prevent stuff like this happening. And how those could scale. Nationally. Globally, even.

ASAF. Yeah this is definitely the same Nakia Clark.

BARON. What? Oh. Yeah, it's a lot. I was like: "*Damn*, some of this wasn't even on my radar." But the *hope* is Deronte's case could be a tipping point. *Here*, anyway. Cuz the cops that did it? *Nothing's* happened to them. I mean they're on, you know, "paid administrative leave" and supposedly a grand jury's deciding if to indict, but no one's, like, *optimistic*. Cuz between the DA and the police, everybody has to stay friends, right? So. What we're doing right *now* is, basically, collecting signatures.

ASAF. Oh! *(Holding out his hand for the document –)* Of course, lemme –

BARON. Really? Cool.

ASAF. Of *course*.

> *(**BARON** hands the document to **ASAF**, who starts to flip through it. Meanwhile –)*

BARON. Well you'd be surprised. Or maybe not. I mean, there's a lotta support in the city. *And* from students. Mostly. But the suburbs? Professor's Hill?

ASAF. Yeah that's where I live.

BARON. Exactly. So, we're targeting people more directly where we have, you know, personal relationships. Hence my coming to you.

ASAF. Right, and: signing just conveys my support for the demands.

BARON. Yes. *And* we're also planning a march? For whenever the grand jury decision comes down. Which could turn into a protest, depending, so signing is also sort of a pledge to be with us that day. More pressure on them to do the right thing.

ASAF. Right. *(Beat.)* I mean, yeah, sounds great, I'll –

BARON. Cool. Thanks.

ASAF. Definitely. I mean I'll actually want to *read* the thing before I –

BARON. No, sure.

ASAF. – Put my *name* on it, but, yeah, yes, I will...help in any way I can. *(Beat.)* Baron, again, I'm so sorry this happened.

BARON. Thanks. Yeah. *(Beat.)* I mean, he and I were *very* different? We did not, um, *agree* with all of one another's choices. But he had a good heart. And he didn't steal that car.

ASAF. Well and even if he had.

BARON. What?

ASAF. Even if he *had.* If he'd stolen *ten* cars. You don't... execute someone without a trial. Or even *with* a trial. There's no death penalty for stealing cars.

BARON. Right but he didn't.

ASAF. No, I know, I'm just...saying.

(**ASAF** *and* **GWEN**.)

GWEN. Oh god, yeah, that was bad.

ASAF. Yeah.

GWEN. No, and have you seen the video?

ASAF. No, not yet, I'm...gonna, I just –

GWEN. It's bad. He asks what he did and they *instantly*... And then they lied about it for weeks. They're still lying. I mean, it highlights all the legit complaints the community has about the way the area near campus is policed versus...*other* parts of the city. Like: do they send a small *army* if cars are getting stolen downtown? Do the cops even *go* there? But God forbid any full-tuition parent has to worry about the SUV they bought Junior for his eighteenth birthday.

ASAF. Right.

GWEN. Right? *(Beat.)* But, hey: it's great he *came* to you. And that you can be a part of the *solution,* or... Not that there *is* one, or not an *easy* one, but: *you* know what I mean: great that you can *do* something. *(Beat.)* And! Weird coincidence that your ex is the one *running* this, we were just –

ASAF. Yeah. Weird. Yeah.

GWEN. What.

ASAF. Well, um... *(Beat.)* Okay so I read this thing, and it's great, it's...thorough and passionate and intelligent and everything I'd expect from Nakia.

GWEN. *(Slightly threatened –)* Wow, okay.

ASAF. What? No, just... It covers a *lot*. That I *agree* with, ninety, ninety-*eight* percent of it. How, under the incentives of brute capitalism, nothing matters more than profit, not even people, but how the people you can get away with *harming* are whoever's marginalized, so, in large part, black and brown. It's who we jail. It's whose water we fuck up and whose health care we deny. It's who we send to war and who we go to war against. And if support for this ever wavers, we just exaggerate or *invent* the threat that these marginalized people pose, here and elsewhere. And how the *antidote* to this is a systemic overhaul to change the incentives, everything from ending qualified immunity for cops to reallocating military and police funding to things like jobs, mental health, education. I know you *know* all this, I'm just setting the –

GWEN. Yeah.

ASAF. Right, but: there's *one* section, about America's involvements *overseas*, which, well, listen: *(He reads –)* "The United States must also end all military aid to and impose sanctions on the apartheid state of Israel until it ends the settler-colonialist oppression of the Palestinians through its ongoing occupation of the West Bank, blockade of Gaza, and refusal to recognize any right of return for the refugees of 1948."

GWEN. Okay. *(Beat.)* And you *disagree* with that.

ASAF. I, well, *no*, not *mostly*. I *oppose* the occupation. I always *have*. It's why my parents *left*! Or, *that's* not true cuz they left before it started, but it *continuing* is at least *partly* why they never went back, and the *settlements* are a...*kind* of colonialism. And the blockade... I mean: you hear stuff that's just inhumane. And, as for the refugees, I mean... Between *us*, I don't see that *happening*. But doesn't mean they don't have a *point*. And the United Sates is complicit in *all* these things, yeah, through aid, military and otherwise.

  (Beat.)

GWEN. So you *agree*.

ASAF. Well, not *entirely*, cuz... Well, first of all I don't know if I'd use the word "apartheid"? Just cuz I don't think you can go around plucking terms from one historical moment and dropping them into others like they *apply*. Though, on the other hand, if what's meant is just different laws for two groups of people, based sort of on ethnicity, within areas *one* mainly *controls*, it might, as analogies go, be the best we have.

GWEN. Okay. So –

ASAF. And, hang on, while I can see the need, given the *extreme* rightward tilt of Israel's leading politicians *lately,* for pressure to move the needle back towards creation of a Palestinian state? Which of course I *also* support? And while divestment and sanctions are legitimate tools for *applying* that pressure – non-violent ones, which is *great* – doing it unilaterally, overnight doesn't strike me as sensitive to the complexities of a region where *many* groups contribute to what's happening.

GWEN. Oh...kay –

ASAF. Well but the *real* problem... And, again, this is like a twenty-page document. And what struck me as sort of weird is that Israel is the *only country* mentioned. In this way.

GWEN. Huh.

ASAF. Yeah. *(Beat.)* What I mean is other countries are *mentioned*? But in the context of America doing terrible things there. But *Israel* is the *only country* whose *own policies* are condemned, where it says *not* "we shouldn't be involved there cuz of what *we* do" but rather "we shouldn't be involved cuz of what *they* do."

GWEN. Right.

ASAF. Well don't you think that's weird? That it doesn't say...stop aid to India over Kashmir, or how they treat *their* Muslims? Or sanction China over Tibet, or Taiwan, or the Uyghurs –?

GWEN. I'm pretty sure we *did* sanction China.

ASAF. Or Turkey cuz of the Kurds! Or a...dozen other examples. Argentina.

GWEN. Yeah, no, I guess. *(Beat.)* Huh.

ASAF. What.

GWEN. No, just… First of all, I didn't realize you felt so strongly about this.

ASAF. About what?

GWEN. So…*defensive* of Israel.

ASAF. I *don't* feel *so*… I'm not *saying*… No. *I'm* just defensive of…internally consistent *logic*.

GWEN. Okay.

ASAF. Yeah which this document seems to *lack* on this one subject.

GWEN. Okay. Cuz it would make sense if you *did*. Feel defensive. Your parents *are* from there. They may have *left* but they're *from* there. *Most* of your relatives still live there. You're a *citizen*.

ASAF. Yeah cuz they're desperate for more of us. And my dad's *barely* from there: his father dragged the family back to Europe when he was a kid.

GWEN. Well, and: remember your twenty-year reunion? That old roommate of yours, works for a hedge fund or something, had just come back from like a *week* in South Korea, so was *holding forth* on how the media there fearmongers about mad cow or whatever, and I bit his head off?

ASAF. Yeah, sorry, that guy's an asshole.

GWEN. Yes. But the *point* is: this is *your* tribe.

ASAF. No, I hear you, I just – and it's twelve tribes, but – I'm not, I've never *been*, like, a "mob enthusiasm" person. I find it embarrassing if not scary. I can't even really cheer at *sporting* events.

GWEN. Weren't you *in* a Jewish youth group?

ASAF. Yeah in Northern Cali*forn*ia. We practiced the acoustic-*guitar*-based variety of Judaism, where you go into the *woods* and sing egalitarian versions of the prayers and try to hook up with girls from the Central Valley named, like, Serena, it wasn't –

GWEN. Fine, I'm just saying it wouldn't be weird or unusual if you felt –

ASAF. *(Snapping –)* Yeah but I *don't*!

GWEN. I...stand *corrected.*

ASAF. I... Look. My "feelings" about Israel are the... *reasonable* ones.

GWEN. Which are?

ASAF. That there were strong arguments for creating it, so it's maybe good that it exists, but that I *don't* like a lot of things it actually *does.*

GWEN. Okay. *(Beat.)* So to clarify: you don't disagree with the actual *criticisms.*

ASAF. I... *No*, I don't think so, not mostly.

GWEN. You just disagree with Israel being singled out like this.

ASAF. I... I mean, yeah, I guess I do.

GWEN. Okay –

ASAF. And even if I *did*! Even if I *do*...disagree with *some* of the criticisms, the, the *freedom to criticize*, itself, is... If someone said these things in a context where criticism of Israeli policy was the *actual subject*, I'd be *fine* with that, but, framed like *this*...

GWEN. Right. *(Beat.)* And so are you really thinking of not *signing* it now, or –?

ASAF. Well –

GWEN. Cuz this kid, Baron –

ASAF. No, I *know*.

GWEN. Right? Won't that seem *petty*, in the face of...? Plus... *(Beat.)* And look: this is kind of neither here nor there? But at this *particular* moment, for *me*?

ASAF. What.

GWEN. Well... *(Beat.)* Never mind, it doesn't matter.

ASAF. No, what.

GWEN. Well: I'm in the middle of negotiating this deal. Between *that* neighborhood and the school so it's... kinda delicate.

ASAF. You said the meeting went well.

GWEN. Yeah but the last time the university did this in like, the '60s? They did *not* do a good job of...let's just say "preserving local culture." And it left a pretty bad taste. So, yeah, I made promises, but if the *next thing* people see is *my husband*, on this *other issue of importance* to them, taking what will at least *appear* to be the opposing *stance* –

ASAF. Right, right.

GWEN. Right? So: I'm not telling you what to *do*. But if *one sentence* is your only problem with a, like you said, a *twenty-page* document, then maybe –

ASAF. Well, except there is one other thing.

GWEN. What? What.

ASAF. They use the word genocide.

GWEN. What?

ASAF. It *also*... Here: *(He reads –)* *"Failure* to do so will leave the United States complicit in the ongoing genocide of the Palestinian people." Which, again, so much of what happens there is terrible, truly. But: *genocide*? *That's* a term you *really* can't just throw around. *Especially*... Well: you know.

GWEN. Right. *(Beat.)* But if *two* sentences are your only prob–

ASAF. Gwen!

GWEN. What? I'm just –!

ASAF. I *know* but...! Look it's not like I signed *already* and now I'm *withdrawing* my support. No one even knows I'm... No one's gonna look at a list of hundreds of names and go, "Where's Asaf Sternheim?" No one will *care*.

GWEN. Your *student* knows. He knows he asked and that you said you would.

ASAF. I *also* said I had to *read* it first.

GWEN. No, I know, just... No, like I said: do what you think is right.

ASAF. Look, I haven't actually... *(Beat.)* Obviously I'd *like* to be able to sign it. I just have some *questions*. *(Beat.)* Maybe I should just ask my questions.

> (**ASAF** *and* **NAKIA**. **BARON** *is also here, working on a laptop.*)

NAKIA. Asaf Sternheim.

ASAF. Nakia Clark.

> *(They hug sort of awkwardly.)*

NAKIA. What's it been, like fifteen years?

ASAF. Twenty. But you look exactly the same.

NAKIA. What? God, I hope not.

ASAF. No, I just mean: you look great.

NAKIA. Thanks. You too. And I take it you already know Baron?

ASAF. Yeah. *(To* **BARON** *–)* Hey.

BARON. Hey.

NAKIA. I've roped him into handling our web presence. We've learned it's best to let the young people handle the online stuff.

ASAF. You're in good hands. He was my star pupil.

BARON. All right, everybody settle down.

NAKIA. That is so wild. Small world!

ASAF. Yeah. *(Beat.)* So how've you *been*? What've you –

NAKIA. *Oh.*

ASAF. – Been *up* to the last, yeah, decade or two?

NAKIA. I mean basically *this,* in one form or another. Since law school.

ASAF. Great. And it's been...good?

NAKIA. It's been rewarding. But challenging. Especially at times like this. But it's good to be doing it *here.*

ASAF. Right! Are your folks still nearby, or...? *(To* **BARON** *–)* You know, her dad was a big deal professor here.

BARON. What? Really?

NAKIA. He was a *professor*. History. *(To* **ASAF** *–)* But, no, they moved when he retired. Somewhere warmer. How 'bout you? What have you been up to?

ASAF. Oh, I mean: writing, mainly. *(Indicating* **BARON** *–)* Now teaching. Which is yeah, rewarding. Challenging.

NAKIA. Nice. Yeah, I remember a lot of plays about... England and Russia in, like, the seventeen and eighteen hundreds.

ASAF. Heh. Yeah, I was...young.

NAKIA. Right. And you followed your wife here, right?

ASAF. What? Oh –!

NAKIA. Sorry, just: when they created that position, um: "Community Outreach –"

ASAF. "Administrator for Community Relations and External Affairs."

NAKIA. That's the one. There was a *press* release. And I saw who she was married to and was like: oh!

ASAF. Yeah, that's me!

NAKIA. How'd you two meet? You start...showing up at University Administrator events, or –?

ASAF. Ha! No, that...kind of stalking's a young man's game. No, we got set up by mutual friends. But they were smart, they tricked us, invited us both to a thing where we were the only two single people, but didn't tell us it was a set-up? Later they told us they were just tired of hearing us each complain about the intense, unstable people we were dating like *we* weren't the ones *choosing* it and...decided to choose for us. *(Beat.)* I don't mean *you.* I mean later, I –

NAKIA. *(Conscious of **BARON** –)* It's fine.

ASAF. Oh. Yeah. Anyway... Then we got married, and then she got this job.

NAKIA. And how's she handling it?

ASAF. Being married to me? It's tough. No, um, you know: it's...delicate –

NAKIA. Yeah, they really dropped her in it. *(To **BARON** –)* You know your school's trying to take over more of the city.

BARON. *(Steadfastly focusing on the laptop –)* Hey I just *go* there.

ASAF. Well, but –

NAKIA. *(Back to **ASAF** –)* Yeah, this time they're gonna do it nice, right? Cuz you know what happened *last* time.

ASAF. Yeah, I mean: let's just say they didn't do the best job of "preserving local culture," right?

NAKIA. I mean you...*could* put it like that. *(To* **BARON** *–) You* know about Bottomville. Right?

BARON. *(Uncertainly –)* Um –

NAKIA. *("Unacceptable.")* Uh-uh. No. There used to be a neighborhood, south of campus, called "Bottomville." Great Migration town. *Nice.* Families. Businesses. People left doors unlocked. This is the late '50s. But the city wanted the school to be able to expand and you can't just *do* that if a place is *nice.* You need it to be neglected, dilapidated. Dangerous. So they colluded with the landlords, who were white, to raise rents 'til folks had to move *out*, and then didn't move anybody else *in*. Pretty soon you've got abandoned buildings, boarded up businesses, unemployment, crime, 'til *one* day a student who was renting an apartment out there got *stabbed*. At which point, the city, shocked at these terrible new conditions that had mysteriously arisen, commissioned a study, which, lo and behold, showed that Bottomville was now neglected and dilapidated and all the things they needed it to be in order to bulldoze and start over. And now they want to do it again, in *your* neighborhood.

BARON. Yeah, I heard that.

ASAF. *(Lamely –) Yeah* but, like you said, this time they're trying to do it...*well... (Beat.)* How 'bout you, you seeing anybody?

NAKIA. No. So what brings you here today, Asaf?

ASAF. Right, um... *(He hesitates. Then plows ahead –)* Okay, so: I *read* this.

BARON. *(Seeing something on his laptop screen –)* Shit.

ASAF. *(Thinking* **BARON** *is anticipating his question –)* What? No, I'm just –

NAKIA. *(Not confused in the way that* **ASAF** *is –)* What is it.

BARON. *(Turning the laptop towards* **NAKIA** *–)* I mean...

NAKIA. *(Seeing the screen –)* Goddammit. Is this one of the ones you talked to?

BARON. I talked to her *yesterday.*

ASAF. *(Realizing this is not about him –)* Wait, what. What is it.

NAKIA. We're...having some trouble with the media.

BARON. They keep using this photo. For articles about Deronte? This one photo that we keep asking them not to use.

ASAF. Oh. Well, I'm sure... Oh my god.

> *(Because* **BARON** *has turned the laptop to face* **ASAF.***)*

BARON. Yeah. Like he's fucking Scarface.

NAKIA. And we try to get ahead of it. Give them ones where he looks...like he looked, with his friends, with his mom, but they never use those.

ASAF. Right. Shit.

NAKIA. Yeah. *(To* **BARON** *–)* How's the article?

BARON. Ha. *(Reading –)* "But Lee was no angel."

NAKIA. Goddammit.

BARON. *(Reading –)* "He had multiple suspensions from school and was known to scrawl rap lyrics in a journal."

ASAF. Jesus Christ.

> *(A beat. Then –)*

BARON. *(To* **NAKIA** *–)* So what do you want to do?

NAKIA. There's a template letter to the editor on my computer. Then make more calls, to some of the smaller papers. We'll try to get something better into one of them.

BARON. On it.

(**BARON** *exits with his laptop.*)

NAKIA. Great kid.

ASAF. Yeah.

(*Beat.*)

NAKIA. So, sorry, yes, finally: *what* did you want to *talk* about?

ASAF. Oh! I, um, just... (*Pause.*) I just wanted to tell you in person that I support what you're doing.

NAKIA. Oh!

ASAF. And, yeah, that it's really great to see you still committed to this after all these years and I, um... That I'm in!

NAKIA. Really?

ASAF. Yeah. Put me on the list.

NAKIA. *Thank* you.

ASAF. It's... What? No. It's nothing.

NAKIA. No, having people like you involved really does make a difference.

ASAF. Heh, I don't know about *that*, I'll be...*one* name among hundreds. Maybe *thousands*, by the time –

NAKIA. God willing.

ASAF. Right? We'll see if anyone even notices I'm there, heh. (*Beat.*) But so, you knew I was in town?

NAKIA. What?

ASAF. Nothing. Never mind.

(**ASAF** *with* **RACHEL** *and* **FARID**.)

RACHEL. Professor Sternheim? I'm Rachel Klein.

ASAF. Hello.

RACHEL. And this is Farid El Masry.

FARID. Hey.

ASAF. Hi.

RACHEL. Is this a bad time?

ASAF. No I um... Come on in.

RACHEL. Great, thanks. It's great to meet you. We're big fans.

FARID. *(Trying to head off confusion –)* Oh. Um –

ASAF. You know my work?

RACHEL. Work?

ASAF. Oh, just –

FARID. *(To **RACHEL** –)* Yeah, he's also a writer.

RACHEL. Oh! Right. Of course, I knew that.

ASAF. Yeah. That's...okay.

RACHEL. Yeah, no, but I meant: we're fans of the very public stance you've taken.

ASAF. Oh.

RACHEL. Yeah. *(Beat.)* Sorry, do you know what this is about?

ASAF. I...have an inkling? But –

RACHEL. Oh, sorry! Let me back up. *(To **FARID**.)* Or, do you wanna –?

FARID. No, you go ahead.

RACHEL. Okay. *(To* **ASAF.***)* So. *I* am, or more accurately *was*, a member of the campus chapter of the Jewish Student Union. And Farid is a member of Students for Palestinian Justice.

FARID. *(Making fake "scary" hands –)* Rarr! Kidding.

ASAF. Heh.

RACHEL. Yeah. And a *while* ago we tried to organize a joint event. We were going to invite a speaker to campus: Dr. Isaac Roth. Heard of him?

ASAF. No.

RACHEL. Oh. *(Then, to* **FARID** *–)* How would you –?

FARID. He's an expert on the Middle East.

RACHEL. Yeah, and Israel-Palestine in particular: he's studied it *literally* all his life. And we *were* gonna have him give a talk, do a Q&A, and we, meaning JSU, were gonna co-sponsor this with SPJ. Turns out, though, that we're not *allowed* to.

ASAF. Why?

RACHEL. *Well*: *first* of all because Isaac Roth – who's Jewish, incidentally, in case you couldn't tell – apparently violates some policy none of us were aware of? But that was established at the top, which is to say by the national *umbrella* for JSU under which –

ASAF. Sure.

RACHEL. Which *states*, apparently, that no chapter is allowed to host a speaker who… Okay, so the actual *language* is something like, "Who calls for the destruction of the State of Israel"?

ASAF. Well –

RACHEL. Right, but the way they *interpret* that is so *broad* it amounts to, you know, "Anyone who levels any criticism at Israel at *all*." *And* none of that even really *mattered* because it *also* turned out we were banned from co-sponsoring *any* event with SPJ because the national organization has *them* on a list of groups that, quote, "call for the destruction of Israel," which, guess what, they don't.

ASAF. Right. *(Then, to* FARID *–)* You don't, right?

FARID. No, we...call for Palestinian autonomy over Palestinian land.

ASAF. Right. I mean I...agree with that.

RACHEL. Yeah, we *know,* that's why we're *here.*

> *(She takes some paperwork out of her bag.)*

See at first we were thinking maybe SPJ could just go ahead and host the event on their *own* and whoever wanted to from JSU could just show up. But that would send the wrong message, like: it would support this insane idea that saying anything other than "Israel is awesome" is somehow out-of-bounds for Jews. *And* it would make the event easy to *dismiss* as just a hostile act by Arab or Muslim students.

ASAF. *(Understandingly, to* FARID, *perhaps echoing his "scary hands" gesture –)* Right.

> *(*FARID*'s like, "It is what it is.")*

RACHEL. Right, which is why we *realized* that what we *really* needed was to form a totally new organization, *specifically* for Jewish students who want to get out from under this policy and use *that* organization to co-sponsor the event as we originally planned. But to do *that*: we need someone from the faculty to sponsor us.

ASAF. *(Getting it –)* Ohh.

RACHEL. Yeah! Honestly, I'm a little embarrassed we didn't think of you right *away*. I mean before we saw your name on the Lee Manifesto.

ASAF. Right. Yeah.

RACHEL. But when we talked, in the abstract, about who this person ought to be *and* what kind of person was likely to say yes we were basically describing you.

ASAF. As...what?

RACHEL. Young, Jewish, progressive, and cool.

ASAF. *(Flattered –)* Oh. *(Beat.)* I mean I'm not...*that* Jewish.

FARID. Heh.

RACHEL. What?

ASAF. Nothing. Go on?

RACHEL. Oh well that's sort of it, that's sort of the pitch.

FARID. Yeah and: to be clear, this kinda thing's *not* a huge time commitment. We know you're busy so –

ASAF. *("Not really.")* Well –

FARID. – It could honestly *just* be signing the form.

RACHEL. Right, you wouldn't have to actually *preside* over our meetings and help us *plan* things. Though, if you *did* want to be involved in that way, we'd obviously welcome that as well.

ASAF. Right. *(Beat.)* And the idea would be to invite this guy to campus, this –

RACHEL. Dr. Roth.

ASAF. Right and: let him talk.

RACHEL. I mean for *starters*, yeah, though once we're not bound by this stifling *policy* anymore there's all *kinds* of things we could do.

FARID. You can do whatever your consciences demand.

ASAF. Right, which is always...good.

RACHEL. Uh, *yeah*. *(Beat.)* Is that a yes?

ASAF. Um –

FARID. Mm.

> (**RACHEL** *subtly gestures and murmurs something to* **FARID**, *something like, "Just a sec."* **FARID** *shrugs and murmurs back, "I didn't say anything." This happens very quickly and* **ASAF** *doesn't quite catch it.)*

ASAF. What?

RACHEL. Nothing. Go on.

FARID. Yes. Please.

ASAF. Okay. *(Beat.)* I mean, yeah: I was just gonna ask if there's somewhere I can look at the kinds of things this guy *says*, like –

RACHEL. Oh.

ASAF. – Articles or speeches... I mean just cuz literally *all I know* about him is what you just told me which is that he's banned for "calling for the destruction of Israel."

RACHEL. Yeah but as I expl–

ASAF. Which, no, I'm sure is a gross distortion and exaggeration but I'd still like to see for myself what we're actually talking about before I, you know –

RACHEL. Right, no, of course, I mean you can just...google him and find articles or go on YouTube and watch speeches he's given elsewhere.

ASAF. Great. I will.

RACHEL. But, first of all, what you'll see is that he's not saying anything all that egregious or even controversial?

ASAF. Great. I'll take a look.

RACHEL. And but *beyond* that... I mean we can argue where the line is and what position does or doesn't cross it, but this is about something bigger to me. I mean leaving aside that *banning speech* is counter to academic freedom and therefore a weird thing to be doing on a university campus? It *also* doesn't seem particularly...

ASAF. What.

RACHEL. *Jewish*. To me. *(Beat.)* I mean, first of all, Jewish ethics *commands* us to fight injustices when we see them. "She who can protest but does not is accomplice in the act."

ASAF. Right. Very Talmudic.

RACHEL. Yeah it's...from the Talmud.

ASAF. Oh.

RACHEL. Yeah. *And* when we invoke the, sort of, post-Holocaust **mandate Never Again?** That means Never Again for *anyone*. Not just us.

ASAF. Well, right, but –

RACHEL. And and but *beyond* all that: I don't know about you but to *me* Judaism has always been *about questioning*. You know? About *wrestling* with the big ethical and moral quandaries of the day and then admitting none of us really *knows* the answer. It's a whole religion *built* on questions, or at least I *thought* it was: we argue about everything, even with ourselves. Get two of us in a room, you get four opinions. It's the thing that made me proudest to be a Jew. Look at the Talmud! There's the text, and the commentary, and the commentary on the commentary, *generations* of Rabbis disagreeing with each other like a, a, culture-wide *bathroom* stall! And when you *study* the Talmud, in Yeshiva? They have you do it in pairs and *tell* you to disagree! They *literally assign* you someone to *argue* with, it's called a chavruta partner! *That's* the spirit of the Judaism I grew up with, the Judaism I grew up loving, not this authoritarian, doctrinaire, "There's one correct opinion and everything else is not allowed." Not to mention the irony of *Jews* putting *other* people – Jews *included*! – on *lists* for their beliefs. So, whatever you think of Dr. Roth, *that's* really what I'm, what we're trying to preserve: Judaism's grand intellectual tradition of not knowing anything for sure.

(**ASAF** *and* **GWEN**.)

GWEN. So you're thinking of *doing* this.

ASAF. Well I looked the guy up and...I mean, he's *provocative*, sure, he says things that make me *really uncomfortable*, but nothing you could *remotely* construe as "calling for the destruction of Israel." At least *I* didn't think so. On the *contrary*, his thing is: "I'd like to *save* Israel but if we're going to *do* that there's certain things we need to con*front*.

GWEN. Okay.

ASAF. (*Musing –*) Yeah, I don't know, he's interesting. Yeah. (*A beat. Then –*) Like, okay, for *decades* Israel's borders kept *expanding*, right? And the conventional wisdom, or, you know, what *I* was taught, even in my liberal Bay Area Jewish education, was: well, they kept *winning* defensive *wars*. *This* guy asks: what if those wars weren't totally *defensive*? What if aspects were *avoidable* but entered into anyway *because* the likely outcome was more territory? Like with '48. What *I* learned was: the British pulled out, the Arabs rejected partition and invaded, and told local *Palestinians* to leave and come back when Israel was destroyed. But when Israel *won*, those Palestinians got stranded outside the Green Line, to which Israel just *happens* to have expanded. *This* guy's like: come *on*, people, that was the *goal*. Israel pushed most Palestinians out *themselves. The war* just gave them cover to *do* it. Or with '67. What *I* learned was: Israel was *forced* to launch a preemptive strike to prevent *another* invasion and just sort of ends up with the occupied territories. *This* guy says Israeli and American intelligence *both thought* it *very unlikely* the Arabs would actually attack and that, if they *did*, Israel would win easily. There was apparently a *meeting* about it where the CIA was like, "They can't beat you and they know it," and the Israelis were like, "Yeah we know." And then attacked first *anyway* and... Well, on the seventh day, they rested. And so on, about...*most* wars Israel's ever fought.

GWEN. Okay.

ASAF. Well, and so, his point, as I understand it, is a kind of *reframing*, to say: maybe if Israel keeps gaining more territory it's not because they're *unwilling recipients* of it but rather cuz they just *want* more *territory*, which might be worth keeping in mind in light of their *current* argument that they can't return any territory they still occupy on the grounds they'll be *attacked* again when maybe who attacked who in the first place isn't so clear.

GWEN. Right. *(Beat.)* And you *agree* with all that.

ASAF. I don't know! On the one hand, Israel *has* offered territory back in exchange for peace and, when it's *gotten* it, it's *given* it back, like with Egypt, and sometimes even when it *hasn't*, like with Gaza. But, on the other hand, the Six-Day War *was* preemptive, and the idea that *hundreds of thousands* of Palestinians just left *voluntarily* in '48 because Arab armies *told* them to was always sort of an Israeli national *myth*. What actually *happened* was way more complex.

GWEN. Right. Okay, so... *(Beat.)* Sorry, *what* are you saying now?

ASAF. I'm saying he makes some good points and other points I question but that whether I *totally agree* with *this specific guy* or not I *definitely* think banning people *like* him from even *talking* makes the pro-Israel crowd look *terrible* by confirming everybody's worst suspicions about them.

GWEN. Does this have to do with your ex-girlfriend?

ASAF. What? *(Beat.)* What? What do you...? *What?*

GWEN. I don't know! You have a strong opinion one way and then –

ASAF. It wasn't *that* strong!

GWEN. And then you talk to *her* for five minutes and not only do you sign the thing you didn't want to sign –

ASAF. *You* wanted me to sign it!

GWEN. Oh, hey, no, it's great for *me*. I'm just trying to figure out how you ended up *running* an organization dedicated to the opposite point of view of the one you used to have.

ASAF. It's...! Okay *first* of all I'm not *running* it. They just need, like, a grown-up to sign off so they can run it themselves. *Secondly* –

GWEN. I'm just –

ASAF. Lemme finish. *Secondly*: it's not dedicated to the "opposite point of view" of *anything*. It's *expanding* the number of points of view that are *allowed*. Thirdly this has nothing to do with Nakia. She doesn't even *know* about it. These kids approached me on their own.

GWEN. I, yeah, I understand all that. What I'm *saying* is it just seems a little weird to me. Like maybe...

ASAF. What.

GWEN. You're trying to impress her.

ASAF. I just *told* you –

GWEN. Yeah but she's gonna find *out*, right? She will *become aware of it* if you *do* this. That is a thing that will happen, right? I... Look, I'm not trying to change the subject.

ASAF. I no longer know what the subject *is*.

GWEN. When we have sex... *(Beat.)* Look, I've said this before. *Sometimes* it's like you're not totally *there*.

ASAF. Right. *(Beat.) What* does that mean again?

GWEN. That some part of you is held back! Outside it somehow. I don't know how else to explain.

ASAF. Okay, because, in *fact*, I *am* there.

GWEN. I'm not saying you're not *good* at it. You're very *invested* in being good at it, the way you are in being good at *everything*. But, anyway, since we *moved* here, and her *name* started coming up –

ASAF. You're the one who keeps bringing her up!

GWEN. *I've* just been feeling a little insecure, okay? About, whether, when you're *elsewhere*, in your *head*...where else you might be.

ASAF. Meaning with *her*. *(Off* **GWEN***'s shrug* –*)* Okay, well, you really really *really* don't need to worry about that, okay?

GWEN. No?

ASAF. No, it's... *First* of all: I love you. And I do not think about anybody else.

GWEN. Okay. *(Beat.)* I mean you're allowed to...*think* –

ASAF. Well, and, in any case, let's just say there's good reasons that that relationship didn't work out. And that we then didn't speak for twenty years.

GWEN. Wow, okay. *(Beat.)* Except now I'm pretty curious about *those*.

ASAF. About what. Why.

GWEN. Why am I curious about what went *so wrong* between you and another woman that you didn't *speak* for twenty years?

ASAF. I mean it doesn't... It's not anything that has relevance to *us*.

GWEN. Great, so it shouldn't be hard to *talk* about. *(Off him –)* No, look, I'm just realizing you haven't *really* told me what happened with you two and I always assumed it was cuz it wasn't that big of a deal. But *now* I'm starting to wonder if, actually, it's cuz it *was*.

> *(Beat.)*

ASAF. I'll tell you what happened.

GWEN. Okay tell me what happened.

ASAF. So Nakia's Black, as you may have –

GWEN. Yeah, I'd guessed.

ASAF. Not that *that* was the... But we met in a political science class, and I think what I was drawn to... I mean she was *really* smart and passionate and –

GWEN. Uh-huh, you've said.

ASAF. But I think what it was, more than that, was... All these ideas – affirmative action, criminal justice reform, marijuana legalization... Like: I knew what *side* of them I was on, and I'd take that side in arguments, and since I was by then *voting*, I would vote for them, but that was sort of the extent of it, they were abstractions to me, but the way *she* talked about it was...personal, it connected to... The ideas and the lived experience became one. *(Beat.)* Which isn't to say I'd *never* encountered people personally affected by these things, I, of *course* I'd –

GWEN. Right.

ASAF. So the fact that I was also *interested* probably played a part. But it really affected me, and I wanted to get to know her, and so... This is sort of embarrassing, but I started *going* to things, meetings, protests, things I knew she was involved in – not that it was *fake*, these were all, like I said, positions I actually *supported*, I'd just never gone beyond that to actual *activism*, and she, and the people I encountered *through* her, really opened my eyes because – because this was the late '90s? So we're in Bill Clinton's second term and we liberals, or I should say *white* liberals, have a tendency to get kind of complacent when we have power, like, "Oh, our guy's in, I guess everything's fine." But she, and her circle, were already – cuz they were the *victims* of it – sort of hip to the neo-liberal **bait-and-switch** that was kind of Clinton's whole thing. Like the mandatory minimums in his crime bill or asking why he'd intervened in the Bosnian genocide but not the Rwandan one. And I'm from Berkeley, I thought I *was* a lefty but they, *she*...pulled me left. *(Beat.)* And then we graduate, and it's 2000 and George W. Bush wins – or rather "wins" – and everything got very intense.

GWEN. You weren't lefty *enough*.

ASAF.   No, it wasn't *that*. We protested ending the recount together, and Bush's stupid tax giveaway to the rich, and his stem cell idiocy. But then... *(Beat.)* Well then the World Trade Center came down. And that was traumatizing. I mean for the whole country, sure, but especially if you were in New York that day, in Manhattan, I mean they closed everything, all the bridges and tunnels, so you couldn't get off the island. We all went and tried to give blood and they didn't *need* any because nobody was wounded. Everybody was just dead. So we went and sat in Central Park – it was the most beautiful day – and there were F-16s circling overhead. *(Beat.)* But it wasn't like we split on the politics then either. I mean, even in our shock and grief, we could *see* how American policy had at least set the *table* for something like that, and *especially* once it became clear they were just gonna *use* it, this *tragedy*, to create a surveillance state while waging endless war, we protested that too, we were in the streets, and got called un-American, or...French, for some reason. *(Beat.)* But, turns out, in my *relationship* what I wanted was for us to be extra *nice* to each other. In private, interpersonally: understanding, and flexible and...*nice*. And she sort of...went the other way. She got harsh, impatient. Little stuff. This is so stupid, but I remember: we were out to dinner and she got a pasta dish with shrimp and they came as, like, whole shrimp, with the heads on and everything. And I was like, "Wow, those shrimp are crazy looking." And she was like, "That's what shrimp look like." Like what I'd said was the dumbest thing she'd ever heard. And when I tried to point out to her that she had started doing stuff like that she'd get, like, *outraged*. At the idea that she should be at all gentle with me. Or maybe *I'd* become more sensitive because, I started to realize, she'd sort of *always* been that way, with me, unforgiving. I mean, you're worried I'm trying to *impress* her, but the truth is it was *barely possible* to rise up to *not disappointing*. *(Beat.)* And it *was* political, or at least... 'Cause when we talked about it, she'd talk about how, here she is, this Black woman, who the world either shits on or ignores, while the *same* world bends over backwards to handle the feelings of white men with kid gloves, right? And then there *I* am, like, "You're too dismissive of my thoughts on shrimp, be nicer." So she was just like, "I do this all day, every day. For, like, my *safety*. I have to do it at home, with you, too?" And I was like, right, but you know where my heart is, you've *seen* all the things I've done, by your side. I just want my girlfriend to be *kind* to me. And it was this...impasse. And then she got into law school and we were like, well, you should go. And I should not go with you. And that was it.

And looking back I still don't know who was right, if I should have been consistent in my politics even within the relationship or if an intimate relationship is a place where politics can't really apply or if the whole thing is just kind of unresolvable, I don't know. We ran into each other once like a year later at a protest against the invasion of Iraq. She was there with her new boyfriend – this guy Tariq who'd been pretty obviously in love with her and fairly hostile to me the whole time we'd been together – and she was like, "Huh. Still at it, I see." Like she really thought the only reason... Like she still couldn't believe that my commitment... That I was genuine.

GWEN. Huh.

ASAF. What.

GWEN. Just "huh."

ASAF. Okay. *(Beat.)* But yeah, so: *obviously* that's not us. I mean you're...*very* patient with me. Understanding. *(Beat.) But, and*: I'll think about what you said, about me being held back, I...don't want you to feel like that.

GWEN. Okay. *(Beat.)* Okay, yeah, so if you're gonna *do* this?

ASAF. What? Oh.

GWEN. Keep in mind that it's kind of a sensitive area.

ASAF. I mean, yeah, you said, but –

GWEN. In the opposite direction. *(Off him –)* There are people with *very strong feelings* about this. Donors. Trustees. Other groups. And there's a difference between being *one* signature on, like you said, a document *mostly* about something *else* and being the grown-up *face* of... *(Beat.)* You know what? Never mind.

ASAF. Um, are you *sure*? Cuz –

GWEN. Yeah, no, you just... Do whatever you think is right.

ASAF. Okay. *(Beat.)* I mean I stood right here, the other day, and said, to you, that if someone were engaging in criticism of Israel, on its own terms, as their actual subject, that I would support that. And then someone drops an opportunity to do that, right in my lap, I just, I think... *(Beat.)* I would be a huge fucking hypocrite if I said no.

(**ASAF** *and* **REUVEN**.)

REUVEN. Professor Sternheim? May I speak with you?

ASAF. Oh, I mean: generally office hours are by *appointment*? So... *(Then, as he just comes on in –)* Or okay just come on in.

REUVEN. I need to speak with you about some very troubling viewpoints that are being encouraged on this campus – biased, misleading, and antisemitic – and with which, to my surprise and dismay, the names of a number of Jews including yours are associated. Do you know of what I speak?

ASAF. You might have to be more specific.

REUVEN. The formation of a new organization –

ASAF. Okay.

REUVEN. – The entire *purpose* of which is to provide a platform on this campus for a man with a history of spreading lies and defamation about the Jewish state and of which you are the faculty sponsor. Is this specific enough?

ASAF. Well I'd describe it *differently* but –

REUVEN. Good. So: this man must *not* be invited to campus, you must withdraw your sponsorship, and this organization must be immediately disbanded.

ASAF. I'm sorry, *who* are you?

REUVEN. My name is Reuven Fisher and I am a PhD candidate in Jewish History and Judaic Studies and also a member of **JSU**.

ASAF. Okay, well, Mr. Fisher, I think you may be overstating things somewhat.

REUVEN. I am relieved to hear it because this means you are merely misguided and not self-loathing but –

ASAF. Okay before we go any further? I'm gonna need you to change your tone.

REUVEN. What? What do you mean?

ASAF. Just, your affect is very confrontational which I think is *rarely* called for? But given that you're a student and I'm faculty –

REUVEN. I thought you were Israeli.

ASAF. What? *(Beat.)* I mean I...have Israeli *parents*, what does that –?

REUVEN. Okay so I am just *talking* and you should *know* it's just talking.

> *(Beat.)*

ASAF. Are *you* Israeli?

REUVEN. No I'm from New Jersey.

ASAF. Okay so then –?

REUVEN. But I have *been* many times, and I *studied* there five years, and my *family... This is just talking,* okay? Don't, don't *distract* by –

ASAF. Fine just please lower your voice a little.

REUVEN. Okay.

ASAF. Okay. Secondly. The *only reason* a new organization is necessary at *all* is because of some ridiculous rule that *bans* certain points of view from –

REUVEN. What ban? Nothing is banned! Not from the universe or even from this campus! The *only thing* the rule prevents is the *major official organization for Jewish students in the nation* from hosting those who would bring about the destruction of Israel and of the Jews. I mean: would you expect the, the *Black* student union to host a speaker from the KKK?

ASAF. Would I *expect* them to? No. But if they *wanted* to –

REUVEN. Why would they *want* to!?

ASAF. I don't know but if they *did* I'd hope they'd be *allowed* to instead of someone in some national office somewhere telling them they *can't*.

REUVEN. You see I disagree. I think certain points of view must by certain communities be considered mi chutz la machaneh.

ASAF. I don't know what that means.

REUVEN. Outside the camp of legitimate opinion.

ASAF. *All* the guy does is question the *motives* behind some of Israel's more aggressive policies. You can't redefine *all criticism* as a call for *destruction*, that's insane.

REUVEN. Hang on. You're not so naïve as to think that these people will walk up to you and say, "Hello I would like please to destroy the Jews." They don't say that. Not everyone is Ahmadinejad. Would that they *were*, they'd be easier to identify! But no, to be so frank is not socially acceptable in the West – at least for *now* – and so *here* the conversation must take place *euphemistically*, in language designed to scramble the brains of well-meaning progressives like yourself: "We just want to ask questions!" Oh, I like questions! "This is in the spirit of open-minded- and inclusiveness!" Oh! I like those things! Thus is the Trojan Horse of antisemitism brought inside the gates. Whether the Isaac Roths of the world *know* this or are merely pawns for the agenda of others is a separate question but also irrelevant because the *effect* is the same.

ASAF. Which is *what*?

REUVEN. To start with? A normalization of hostility towards Jews simply for being Jews. Which we already see! On college campuses in *particular*! Graffiti reading "Zionists should be sent to the gas chamber." Events showing any support for Israel being shouted down and forced to disperse. Hundreds of such incidents, just last year!

ASAF. What, here?

REUVEN. Nationwide.

ASAF. Oh. *(Beat.)* Hundreds of incidents of shouting and graffiti nationwide –

REUVEN. Okay.

ASAF. – How will the Jews ever survive?

REUVEN. This is a joke to you?

ASAF. Not at all. I *definitely* think there are people who want to kill Jews. But from where I'm standing it's not academics wielding rhetoric, or the twenty-year-old progressives inviting them to speak places, it's minor league fascists walking into synagogues with guns.

REUVEN. Then you are standing in the wrong place. Ask yourself: what would be the end result of a global consensus that Israel's security concerns are fabricated? That she has never *really* been threatened but only *pretended* in order to acquire land, not by Hezbollah to the north or Hamas to the south, or by whatever extremist group would fill the vacuum left by withdrawal from Ramallah to the east. Well then her presence in the West Bank is unnecessary, and the blockade of Gaza is unnecessary – indeed a Jewish majority *anywhere* is unnecessary! – and all Israel must do to achieve peace is end these things and all will be well. And because this solution is so obvious, well then, if Israel will not do it willingly then all the people of good conscience of all the nations of the world must come together and apply pressure to *force* her to do it. And what will happen then? Well who among us can predict the future but perhaps we should look at what has happened *every single time* Israel has offered land for peace, from Oslo, to Camp David, to Taba, offered to *divide Jerusalem*, *did* withdraw from Gaza in '05, or Lebanon in '99 where they only were in the first place to *defend* the Lebanese *against* Hezbollah, but never mind that, *every time* the reaction is not the promised peace but more *intifadah*, more rockets, more threats. And so what would be the result of making vulnerable, simultaneously, on three sides *and* from within, to groups dedicated to her destruction, a nation the size of Vermont? Jerusalem would be like Aleppo or Baghdad in a month. The country as a whole would become unlivable. And the Jews of the world would have to return to surviving at the whims of non-Jewish majorities elsewhere, to a climate already sown with hostility against us, and since we all know how well that worked out last time... Well, do you know what "Never Again" means to a Jew?

ASAF. Yes and I thought it meant Never Again for anyone, not just us.

REUVEN. That's right. It means Never Again for anyone. Including us.

ASAF. So *you're* saying we can't even *discuss* how Israel deals with the Palestinians because to do so will trigger a series of events that will lead inevitably to a second Holocaust.

REUVEN. No. What I'm *saying* is the entire so-called "conversation" around this issue is nothing more than propaganda designed to *create the conditions* for a second Holocaust.

ASAF. I think that's alarmist.

REUVEN. And I think the people who sounded the alarm *last* time were *also* told they were being alarmist.

ASAF. Last time we were a tiny minority scattered across Europe! We didn't have an *army*! We didn't have a nuclear *weapon*! This time the *Israelis* are the *majority*, they have the *power*, they –!

REUVEN. Compared to *who*?

ASAF. The Palestinians!

REUVEN. But this conflict is not *between* the Israelis and the Palestinians!

ASAF. *What?* Of *course* it is!

REUVEN. No! It's only *framed* this way so one can conclude that Israel is the oppressor! But this is not now, nor has it ever been, an Israeli-Palestinian conflict in which a Palestinian minority is surrounded by millions of Jews. It is and has always been a Jewish-Arab one in which a Palestinian minority is surrounded by millions of Jews who are themselves surrounded by *hundreds of millions* of other Arabs not to mention the Persians of Iran! Don't you see? This is how antisemitism works! Why it is *invisible* to the left unless someone shouts "kill the Jews" and *sometimes even then*! Because the only xenophobia the *left* understands is the kind that paints the other as inferior. *Jew*-hatred depends upon the opposite: a myth of dangerous *superiority*. "Yes, they are small in number, but they pull all the strings." Antisemitism adopts the trappings of a strike against the powerful so that it can masquerade as part of a struggle for social justice! As a *progressive cause*! So when you say *we* redefine all criticism of Israel as antisemitism you have it *backwards*: antisemitism was *intentionally disguised* as criticism of Israel, by our enemies, *as a response* to the founding of the state! And you can see how effective it has been! It is now impossible for left-wing Western intellectuals to assign *any responsibility at all* to the Arabs for what goes on in a region they dominate completely! But no one *forced* the Arab League to invade in '48, or again in '67 –

ASAF. Well –

REUVEN. Yes, Isaac Roth says it happened differently: maybe we *wanted* them to invade the first time, maybe they weren't *really* going to the second. Let's say he's right! So what? Are the Arabs not still responsible for crossing the border with their armies, or simply massing them there, and screaming that the rivers will run red with Jewish blood? Apparently, Jews are responsible not only for *our* behavior but the Arabs' as well! And let's say Israel used these volatile situations for territorial and demographic advantage. How is this different from every conflict in history? Or *this* one, had it gone differently! You think Egypt, Jordan, and Syria were going to give Palestinians a state? They wanted the land themselves! No one said the *word* "Palestinian"! It didn't *exist* until they needed a new cudgel against *us*! Don't you see what's happening? It's the same old story! France loses a war and, in their desperation to explain it, convicts an innocent Jewish man called Dreyfus. Czarists fearful of the **Bolshevik Revolution** forge a document blaming a global Jewish plot called the Protocols of the Elders of Zion. Communism struggles and the Soviets blame Jewish capitalists while *simultaneously* America is on the hunt for the Jewish communists bringing capitalism down. And so on, from Haman to Hitler, until *now* we are expected to believe that, in one of the most volatile regions of the world, where conflict has raged for thousands of years, the *real source of trouble* is a tiny country that has existed for barely seventy and that *just so happens* to be full of Jews. We are the surface onto which the rest of the world project the ugliest parts of themselves. The funhouse mirror in which they see their own faults, failings, and humiliations. Which is why it has again and again throughout history been decided by otherwise rational men that the way to heal the world, to make it pure, is not to look inward at one's own contribution to suffering – that is too difficult, too complicated – but, rather, simply to rid it of Jews. Only it's not so simple now as it once was, is it, and *that* above all is what the world cannot forgive, that for *once* our destiny is in our own hands and we will not be driven out or murdered. What else explains the title of worst human rights abuser being bestowed upon a country that is for hundreds of miles the only safe haven, not just for Jews, but for Christians, Atheists, women. What else could *possibly explain* the *global hysteria* about a conflict that has claimed fewer lives in its *entire history* than are lost every *six months* now in Syria or Iraq? And when the unthinkable happens, when Israel is as a result of this determination to strip her of all defenses wiped from the face of the earth, tell me that, for this same reason, these same enlightened, liberal, left-wing, progressive Western intellectuals will not have a strange, sneaking suspicion that some way, somehow, even when it came to our own destruction, that the Jews were responsible for this, too. Now why don't you invite a speaker who will ask people all of *that*?

(*A moment.*)

ASAF. Well for one thing JSU *already welcomes* speakers who say that so there's no *need* for me to –

REUVEN. Okay –

ASAF. Look, why don't *you* say all that *at* our event? It's open to anyone. There'll be a Q&A. Why don't you *say* these things, publicly? Have a dialogue?

REUVEN. Because that would lend your event the credence of my presence.

ASAF. You *just said* everyone should look inward! Surely that applies to Jews too. If anything, we have a *special tradition* of considering all points of view on the major moral questions of the day.

REUVEN. What? No we don't.

ASAF. Yes we *do*, we –!

REUVEN. No. Who told you that?

ASAF. Look at the Talmud! Or the...*arguing* partners at *yeshiva*!

REUVEN. Those commentaries were written by the *great Rabbis of history*! The *sages*! I'm sorry, I didn't *realize* you were the reincarnation of Rabbi Akiva and that Rachel Klein was Maimonides or possibly Rabbi Tarfon.

ASAF. All right –

REUVEN. Those men studied the sacred texts all day, every day, for their entire *lives*! Likewise *chavruta* partners in *yeshiva*!

ASAF. Well Isaac Roth has studied the Middle East for *his* entire life, so.

REUVEN. Yes? And what about everyone else in the room? Are they all to be experts as well? And, more importantly, the Talmud, like *chavruta* – and this conversation now! – is an *internal* one amongst *Jews. Your* event is to be, by contrast, a public self-flagellation, a, a *performance* of virtue for the goyim. Professor Sternheim, given what you do for a living, you cannot pretend not to know that the *meaning* of a performance depends *most of all* on who is in the audience.

(Beat.)

ASAF. Well I don't know if you'd call it a *living*, but –

REUVEN. What?

ASAF. Nothing, never mind, so: you accept you can't stop this guy from *talking*. You just don't want any Jews there when he *does*?

REUVEN. *Now* you get it! *Someone* will host this man, it cannot be prevented, fine, I understand, but why must we be complicit in our own demonization?

ASAF. But doesn't the Talmud also command us to fight injustice? Um: "If you see a protest but don't... She who –"

REUVEN. "He who can protest and does not is accomplice in the act."

ASAF. That's the one.

REUVEN. That is what I'm doing! Protesting *your* unjust act, in sponsoring an unjust man, to say unjust things! You are on the wrong side of this. Just as with that manifesto you signed for the Black teenager who stole the car.

ASAF. I... Wait, what?

REUVEN. That, that *document* outlining a plan for remaking the world –

ASAF. I know the one you mean. He didn't steal the car.

REUVEN. Yes he did.

ASAF. No. That's why they *stopped* him, but – have you seen the video?

REUVEN. Yes. I am well aware –

ASAF. But it also doesn't *matter*.

REUVEN. It doesn't *matter*?

ASAF. They shot him, Mr. Fisher. They fucking shot him to death.

REUVEN. *(Backing off –)* Yes, you're right, I understand, I only... *(Beat.)* We Jews *do* have a long history. A special tradition. It is of nodding sympathetically at the unhinged ravings of those who wish us dead. You're a man of principle. And I respect that, I do. But I think you will find that you are being taken advantage of. By people who, in fact, hate you.

(**ASAF** *is alone. Blackout.*)

End of Act One

ACT TWO

*(**RACHEL** and **FARID**, facing the audience.*
***ASAF** watches them, unobtrusively, from*
somewhere off to one side of the audience.)

RACHEL. So: thank you. Thank you to Dr. Roth for a
great talk. Thank you to our audience for such a
stimulating Q&A. And thank you to our allies in SPJ
for co-sponsoring this event.

FARID. Thank you for having us.

RACHEL. Well we...did it together. And thank you *all* for
making this first event hosted by J-FIT – Jews for
Independent Thought – such a success.

(She starts to applaud again but then, cutting
herself off –)

Oh, *and*: if you were inspired by what you heard today,
there is *another* cause, a little closer to home, that
both J-FIT *and* SPJ wanted to bring to your attention.
Baron, did you wanna...?

*(**RACHEL** looks off towards **BARON**, who*
***ASAF** only now notices standing, also*
unobtrusively, off to another side, some
distance from him.)

BARON. Oh, uhhh... I mean, if –

RACHEL. Yeah, come on.

BARON. Okay.

RACHEL. Yeah, just...

(**BARON** *joins* **RACHEL** *and* **FARID** *on stage, standing slightly apart from them.*)

BARON. Okay. Hey, I'm Baron. A lot of you probably don't know me or...maybe you've...seen me around but, anyway, you probably heard about my cousin, Deronte, and what happened to him over the summer and how, since then, there's been no arrest, no indictment, plus a lotta slander from the media. Anyway: I've been involved in a group in the city, Voice to Action, through Nakia Clark – Nakia, you here?

NAKIA. *(Raising her hand –)* Yep!

(**NAKIA** *is, indeed, somewhere here, off to another side.* **ASAF** *is again surprised.*)

BARON. Great. So we've been collecting signatures on her manifesto and also preparing a march for when the grand jury decision comes down and we've got copies here for people to read and a sign-up sheet or you can find it online and add your name there.

RACHEL. Which you *all* should do. *(To* **BARON** *–)* Oh, sorry, were you done?

BARON. No, you're good.

RACHEL. Well, just to say – and obviously everyone should read for themselves and decide, *but* – what Ms. Clark's *brilliant document* lays out is the way in which these different struggles are really all part of the *same* struggle. That if you oppose Israel's settler-colonialist oppression of Palestinians you must also oppose America's oppression of Black **and brown** people here and around the globe and vice-versa. So, again: *read* it, *sign* it if you, you know, aren't a *monster*, and then when the time comes, join Baron and Nakia and their organization in marching on city hall while they join *us* in calling on the university for a total boycott of and divestment from Israel.

ASAF. Oh.

> (**RACHEL**, **BARON**, *and* **FARID**, *and also* **NAKIA** *from wherever she is standing, all look toward* **ASAF** *who has reacted with almost involuntary surprise and discomfort.*)

RACHEL. Professor Sternheim? Something to add?

ASAF. Um... *(Beat.)* No, nothing. Go on.

RACHEL. Oh, well just, be ready cuz: all this could happen soon.

> (**ASAF** *with* **RACHEL** *and* **FARID**. *Nakia's manifesto is on the desk. A beat.*)

Sorry we didn't say anything beforehand but... Well, first of all we weren't sure how much you even wanted to be *involved* –

ASAF. Right, no –

RACHEL. But also it came together really quickly. Like, obviously we'd read the document? It's what *brought* us to you. And *we'd* signed and, you know, people in *our* circle, but it just didn't feel like enough of the campus was paying attention to something that, well, not only happened literally on our *doorstep* but that, frankly, if you think about what happened and *why*, kind of implicates us all.

ASAF. No, sure.

RACHEL. Yeah so we reached out to Baron sort of last second and he was amenable and... As for divestment we figured, likewise, an array of voices would help. Including *yours*, if you –

FARID. Yeah, although that's a *student* vote. It's something we'd be pressuring the *student* government to do, so –

RACHEL. Right, we wouldn't be asking you to *vote* with us. You *couldn't*. Though, if you *did* want to make some kind of public statement of support that is something we would obviously welcome.

ASAF. Right, no, I understand. *(Beat.)* And, look, I'm...a big fan of Nakia Clark. She's an old friend actually.

RACHEL. Wait? Really?

ASAF. Yeah, since we were *your* age: we did marches, protests together –

RACHEL. That's so cool.

ASAF. I just wonder –

(**NAKIA** *and* **BARON** *enter.*)

BARON. Hey, sorry. A *lotta* people wanted to sign the form.

ASAF. Oh!

RACHEL. Yeah I asked them to sit in.

ASAF. Oh. Great! *(To* **BARON** *–)* That's *great*!

NAKIA. Yeah hope that's okay.

ASAF. Yeah no it's... I was just *saying* this is very exciting, getting to work together with...*so* many people I respect.

NAKIA.	**BARON.**
Well: likewise.	Yeah. For sure.

ASAF. Yeah so...

(*Beat.*)

RACHEL. Yeah but it seemed like you also had a question.

FARID. Yes.

ASAF. *Oh*, um... *Well...* (*Beat.*) And, look, this is all great, it's just... If we're gonna fuse all this together, right? Where your manifesto is *our* manifesto and vice-versa, I –

NAKIA. You have a manifesto?

ASAF. I, no, not...*literally,* just –

RACHEL. *("We may have one soon actually.")* Well –

ASAF. Or, what I mean is: if we want to make sure we're making the best possible argument for the...various things we're arguing, then I do, yes, have a couple questions. About what you wrote.

NAKIA.	**BARON.**
Me?	But you...already *signed* it though.

ASAF. Or: I mean I know it's *modeled* on other –

NAKIA. No but I'll take responsibility.

ASAF. Okay.

NAKIA. Yeah. *(Beat.)* So good thing I'm at this meeting then.

ASAF. I was gonna...! Anyway. *(Beat.)* I just wonder. If some of the things in here are entirely fair...

(A moment. Should he? He plows on –)

...To Israel, cuz –

RACHEL.	**FARID.**
What?	Right yeah...

NAKIA. How so?

ASAF. Well –

RACHEL. And Baron's *right*, you already *signed* it.

BARON. I'm just saying.

ASAF. I, well, *yeah*, but there's a difference between being one name *way down* a list and *running an organization* that –

FARID.	**RACHEL.**
You're not running the organization.	You're not running the organization.

ASAF. Yeah, I know, I just: look: when Baron first... Given *everything*, it seemed *petty* and beside the point to... *(To* **RACHEL** *and* **FARID** *–)* And then *you* guys just wanted a space for real *discussion*, which I *also* supported, *do* support, plus obviously I share *many* of your –

NAKIA. *(Flatly –)* So what are your questions?

ASAF. Okay. *First*. I question if it's appropriate to use the word "apartheid."

NAKIA.	**RACHEL**.
Okay.	Whoa, what?

ASAF. Well –

RACHEL. Wait so what are *movement* restrictions? Forced transfers? Let *alone* the territories?

ASAF. Yeah I just mean South Africa was a *very* specific... You know what? Never mind. That's not my main point. And while I respect divestment as a non-violent *tool*... Whatever. Not my main thing either. My *main* thing is. I'm just a little confused by the way Israel *seems* to be... singled out.

NAKIA.	**RACHEL**.
Really.	This is... Wow.

ASAF. I, *yeah*, how you say: "America's guilty of all this stuff. And oh by the way there's *one* other country we want to call out and it's Israel." Because, hang on, I think we can agree the world is *rife* with human rights abuses. But you're not saying divest from India over Kashmir, or China over –

RACHEL. *(Before* **NAKIA** *can reply –)* But this is just whatabouting.

ASAF. What-a...what? What?

RACHEL. It's a tactic people use to prevent anyone ever criticizing Israel. "What about this? What about that?"

ASAF. Oh. Yeah that…sounds annoying. But I'm not saying "don't criticize Israel." I'm just trying to determine the *actual criteria* by which criticism of Israel and *no one else* belongs in this document.

RACHEL. Right. Whatabouting.

ASAF. No.

NAKIA. Well, first of all, we're not *nearly* as bound up with those places, Asaf. I mean, the amount of aid alone –

ASAF. Turkey then. They're a NATO member. Or Egypt! We *pour* money in and let's just say they have human rights issues of their own including, not for nothing, *also* blockading Gaza, from the other *side*.

RACHEL. Right well they're Israel's biggest regional ally.

ASAF. Wait, so – and, seriously, I'm *just* trying to understand – what *most* countries do with American money is America's fault, what *Israel* does with American money is *Israel's* fault, and what *Egypt* does, *also* with American money, is…*also* Israel's fault? Do you see why I'm confused?

NAKIA. Except if you've read the whole *document*.

ASAF. I have.

NAKIA. Then you *know* it's much more specific than "human rights abuses." It's about policies *designed* to harm communities of *color* in the name of *profit*.

ASAF.	**RACHEL**.
Oh. Well –	That's right.

NAKIA. It's about how the intersection of capitalism, colonialism, patriarchy and white supremacy harms us *all*.

RACHEL. *(Snapping her fingers in agreement –)* Yup. That's right. That's right.

NAKIA. *(To* **RACHEL** *–)* Sorry, did you wanna –?

RACHEL. What? No. You go. I'm just –

NAKIA. *(To* **ASAF** *–)* Oh: *and* you're wrong that Israel's the *only* other country we call out. *(Flipping through the document –)* France was until recently engaged in a colonialist enterprise in Mali which we condemned... *(She points –)* ...Here.

ASAF. *(He looks.)* Oh.

NAKIA. Yeah. *(Beat.)* So does that answer your questions? Leaving aside if we need a different *word* for Israel's particular *brand* of apartheid, or –

ASAF. Heh. Right.

NAKIA. – A nonviolent tool *other* than divestment to pursue?

ASAF. Well... *(Beat.)* And, again, I am *with* you on the... overall *thesis*, it's... Hey, you *taught* it to me! Twenty –

NAKIA. C'mon.

ASAF. You did! Twenty years ago! Or I knew *some* things, but you... Anyway. But when you say, for instance, colonialism... And, look, the whole *region* was carved up by *colonialists. And* we can agree Israel is occupying *some* territory it shouldn't. But it's not like the British in India. Right? Or America in...*America.* Or, *yeah*, the French in Mali! Mali's a country France doesn't border in a region to which the French have no historical claim. But Jews didn't show up from some home in Europe to plunder and rule. It *was* home, and they came *back*, cuz they *had* to. *From* all over, by the way, which –

RACHEL. But –!

ASAF. – Hang on, cuz when you say "white supremacy"? Israelis aren't *white.* And I don't mean cuz the Ashkenazim all got tan. There's *millions* of Sephardic Jews, Mizrahi from the Arab world, Ethiopians. They aren't even all Jews! There's Arab Israelis. The point is: *half the country's* Black **and brown** now. *More.* So –

NAKIA. And I take it they're not capitalist or patriarchal either?

ASAF. Oh, no, they're both. *(Beat.)* Though they were officially socialist 'til 1985 and had their first female head of state in 1969. Not important. What I'm saying –

NAKIA. Right, see now *I'm* confused, Asaf. Cuz at *first* it seemed like you were saying we shouldn't single out Israel because, when it comes to systemic oppression, they're nothing special.

ASAF. Well: right.

NAKIA. Yeah but *now* it seems like you're saying we also shouldn't *include* Israel because they *are* special.

    (Beat.)

ASAF. I'm saying it's complicated.

RACHEL. Yeah that's another tactic.

ASAF. What?

RACHEL. Painting the situation as so complicated no one can possibly understand it.

ASAF. I didn't say no one can *understand* it. I said it's complicated because it *is*.

RACHEL. *("Exactly.")* Yeah.

ASAF. I...! Okay. What I'm saying... *(Beat.)* And thank you all, seriously, this is useful, this is clarifying. It's why it's good to talk about this stuff, right? *I'm saying* it's *two* things. It's both. Israel is two different things. *One* is a regional power, backed by Western interests, occupying territory beyond its borders it should return. The *other...* is a *haven*. For a globally persecuted minority, on their ancestral land – not *just* theirs, but also theirs. And the second thing, yeah, *complicates* the first because while, say, leaving the West Bank *is* the moral choice, there is a question of security –

RACHEL.	FARID.
Whoa, *what*?	Okay –

NAKIA. Yeah, that –

RACHEL. We *just got through* listening to an *hour*-long lecture about how that's *not* true. *(To* **NAKIA** *–)* Sorry.

NAKIA. *(To* **RACHEL** *–)* No, you're good.

RACHEL. *(To* **NAKIA** *–)* Yeah, just... *(Back to* **ASAF** *–)* That *you sponsored*!

ASAF. Yeah but I didn't think the takeaway was that Israel's *never* faced any real *threats*.

RACHEL. No it was that Israel has a history of *exaggerating* the threats it faces in order to *justify* seizing *land*.

ASAF. Right, which is an interesting, *provocati...* Okay: what *I* thought we were doing. Was widening our lens to include more points of view. Not *embracing* the next one we *hear* as our new *gospel*. What happened to asking questions? Isaac Roth has *one* framing. A *crucial* one, maybe, but why not *incorporate* it into a, a growing, increasingly *nuanced* –

RACHEL. Yeah this is exactly what people do.

ASAF.	NAKIA.
No.	Okay, look –

FARID. How do you explain the settlements?

> *(A beat as* **FARID** *speaking up, really for the first time, silences everyone. Then –)*

ASAF. Oh. Well, um –

RACHEL. Farid was born there. Gaza. With family in the West Bank.

ASAF. Right, I mean... *(Beat.)* Look, all I'm saying –

FARID. Yes. I heard you, but for fifty years the number of Israelis living on what even *you* acknowledge is occupied Palestinian land has continued to grow. How do you explain it?

ASAF. Okay, well, *no* one in this room is *remotely* in favor of *settlements*, so –

FARID. That's not what I asked.

ASAF. They're...an aggressive right-wing policy designed to make it harder to reclaim land by creating so-called "facts on the ground," yes.

FARID. Left-wing governments built them too.

ASAF. Well, yeah, as a sop to the right to avoid losing power, but –

FARID. If you say so, but if something is the policy of right-wing governments *and* left-wing governments it can't *really* be said to be the "aggressive policy" of a single faction, can it?

ASAF. No, good point, but then the same could be said of *dismantling* them since the left *called* for it and the right *did* it when Sharon left Gaza in '05.

FARID. Yes. I was there. *(Beat.)* And how is Gaza doing now? They immediately blockaded us.

ASAF. Well, but –

FARID. It's a ghetto under siege. No one gets out. And nothing gets *in*: not food, not medicine, nothing but drones and soldiers who come whenever they please to beat and shoot and take people in the night. Into which a nuclear power sends tanks and F-16s to fight boys with rocks. "But"? But *what*?

ASAF. I... *(Beat.)* This is not my point. I *oppose* all that, really, *fervently*, so –

FARID. Okay, but you said "but." But what? I'm curious.

ASAF. But... *(Off the others –) Not* but. *And.* Israel
   didn't blockade *immediately, did* they? They did it
   after Gaza elected Hamas, who *immediately* started
   digging tunnels and firing rockets. I mean how do you
   think Israel ended up with these insane right-wing
   governments in the first place?

FARID. By electing them. Or are Palestinians responsible
   for who we elect as our leaders *and* for who Israelis
   elect as theirs?

ASAF. No, of *course* not, but –

FARID. But?

ASAF. I... No. You know what? We're getting... I'm not
   here to defend any particular *thing* Israel's actually
   done. (Beat. Why is he here? Oh right.) I'm here...
   I signed onto *this* cuz of what happened to Baron.

BARON. *(No one has paid attention to him for some time.)*
   Oh.

ASAF. Right? To your cousin, and the larger pattern
   that's –

BARON. Well, right, but –

ASAF. *(To* **RACHEL** *and* **FARID** *–) And, and, separately,*
   I supported *you* guys cuz *this* conversation, too, is
   really important, and there's voices being stifled in it
   that *shouldn't* be.

FARID. Well –

ASAF. *(Holding up a hand slightly –) But.* I don't *know* if
   these two struggles are actually the same struggle. And
   I just worry – for *you* guys! – that treating them as if
   they *are*, might make *both* harder to win.

BARON. Um –

ASAF. *(To* **BARON** *–)* Right? I mean this must all seem...
   Right? Sorry. You go.

BARON. No, yeah, I've...just been listening cuz, like I said, a lotta this is sorta new to me? And, yeah, at first I wasn't necessarily clocking the connection. But what I'm hearing you say *now* is that, if a disenfranchised minority is being oppressed by military or, say, police violence –

ASAF. Well, hang on –

BARON. – That what they really *ought* to think about is how their own *actions* contribute to that. No?

ASAF. No cuz my whole *point* is it's not the *same*.

BARON. Cuz over *there* the oppressors share an identity with *you*.

ASAF. *No*, cuz...! Well, for one thing, there isn't disagreement here about how many different *countries* this is.

BARON. Ha. You *sure*?

ASAF. I just mean there haven't been an endless series of wars.

BARON. Nope, just *one*, so far. But also: define "wars."

ASAF. I mean you're not *currently firing rockets* at city hall.

BARON. Maybe we should.

ASAF. Maybe you *should* but you're *not* so –

FARID. And Palestinians voted for Hamas because for sixty years we were tricked and lied to and crushed under the boot of the Israelis all while being told, yes, that it was *our* fault for not accepting the crumbs we were offered.

ASAF. What...crumbs? You mean the peace process?

RACHEL. What peace process?

FARID. Yes, what peace process?

ASAF. The one where Israel offered land for peace.

RACHEL. There was never any peace process.

ASAF. What are you...?! There were like *five* of them! A *whole* –

RACHEL. No.

ASAF. *Yes! – series* of increasingly dovish Israeli governments offered more and more up to and including *all* the territories *and* East Jerusalem and *every time* the PLO said no.

RACHEL. Those offers were never serious.

ASAF. That would be news to the people who sacrificed their political and in one case *actual* lives to make them.

RACHEL. Have you actually *looked* at this? Everything important to Palestinians was "to be negotiated later." *Nothing* was guaranteed.

FARID. And why *should* we have to beg for land that was ours to *begin* with?! You agree that the occupation, the settlements, make Israel colonialist. Can you really not see it's colonialist because of the *Nakba*?!

ASAF. Look, what happened in 1948 was, yeah, a *catastrophe*. From your... I *do* see that. *(Beat.)* But that doesn't mean that all of Israel, that the whole *idea* of Israel... *(Beat.)* What are you saying?

FARID. What I'm *saying* is that the first act of aggression in this conflict was the arrival of the Zionists on land that had people *already living on it* with nationalistic ambitions of their own, that the indigenous population responded as anyone would, and that a *real peace* offer would include *full* right of return for *all* refugees *and* their descendants.

ASAF. Which would turn Israel from a Jewish state into an Arab one.

FARID. So?

ASAF. So there's twenty Arab States already and *one* Jewish one.

FARID. So?

ASAF. *So?* Do you know what *happened* to *all the Jews* who used to *live* in those places? Where do you think the Mizrahi *came* from? Communities a *thousand* years old in Syria, Yemen, Iraq, driven out *completely*. So, what, we're just...*trusting* that won't *happen* again, or –?

RACHEL. Actually, many of those communities left voluntarily.

ASAF. Ohmygod.

RACHEL. They *did*! After, like you said, *centuries* of peace, til Israeli aggression turned *some* of their neighbors against them.

ASAF. Yeah? Ask *them* how "voluntary" it was. And how "peaceful" before that.

NAKIA. Yeah, and while you're at it? Ask them how they're doing now. Sorry, can I cut in? Cuz whenever Israel's "diversity" comes up in these conversations I want to ask that next question. Cuz, you know, a country can *be* white supremacist *without* being all white. In fact, it's arguably difficult otherwise. So: do they do as well as the Jews from Europe? Or is this just the demographic equivalent of saying, "But I have Black friends?"

> *(Beat.)*

ASAF. No they don't do as well.

NAKIA. Yes I know.

ASAF. Yeah. *Now* ask me how they vote.

NAKIA. Okay –

ASAF. No, you're right, let's neither of us use millions of brown Jews as a prop. How do they vote? Not all of them, no one's a monolith, but you know that they are, along with the ultra-Orthodox, the most reliable bloc for the Israeli right. Why? Cuz whatever they've suffered at the hands of the Ashkenazi establishment, they know it's *nothing* compared to what they'd face in the Arab world, because they *come* from there and they *remember*. And it's worse *now*. I mean, have *you* looked at what *Islamist* groups say about *Jews*? Let alone women! Homosexuals, getting thrown off rooftops –!

| **FARID.** | **RACHEL.** |
| Um – | Well and *that's* pinkwashing. |

ASAF. *(Loudly –)* Pardon?

RACHEL. Painting Israel as some pro-gay mecca in contrast to the supposedly barbaric Arab nations surrounding it.

ASAF. Okay well I guess everything is called *something* that means you can *dismiss* it without engaging with whether it's *true* or not but come on: there's *millions* of people living under regimes that *execute* you for protesting, and you're just like, "Well that's bad, but at least it's not white-*supremacy* bad, so –"

RACHEL. This is just more whatabouting!

ASAF. *No it isn't!* Not when the thing I'm saying "what about" *is* the *alternative*! Sorry, but if I'm drinking my own urine and the *other option* is *your* liquid shit, it's not whatabouting to say it's *shit*!

FARID. You think Arab culture is shit?

ASAF. *What*? No.

FARID. You think *Arabs* are shit.

ASAF. No because I'm not a *racist* and I'm not talking about actual Arab *culture*. I'm talking about the *ideology* that is right now filling every power vacuum in the region and what I *think* is that oppressive, misogynistic, homophobic *theocracies* are shit no matter who is *running* them! And, before you say it, yes, there are forces in Israel trying to turn it into that right now, into the Jewish *version* of that. But that's *also* why half the country's been in the *streets*, *protesting* –!

FARID. *But where have they been* these protestors? Why are they only *now* in the streets? It's because Netanyahu finally threatens his own *citizens*!

| **ASAF.** | **NAKIA.** |
| I… Well, that's – | Mhm. |

FARID. The Tel Aviv liberals are at long last scared for *themselves*!

ASAF. No, that's a good point, but –

FARID. And the moment they achieve *minimal* protection – apart from a hardy few willing to be treated as *we've* been for years, as the enemy – they will return to sleep, so that the genocide of *my* people can continue. *(A beat. Then, off* **ASAF** *–)* What.

ASAF. Genocide? Really?

FARID. Yes.

NAKIA. Yes.

ASAF. *(To* **NAKIA** *–)* Yes, I know *you* think so, but to describe a conflict in which the total death toll on *both* sides is a few hundred people a year?

FARID. Yes since eighteen-*sixty*! Which is more than a *hundred thousand* people! Civilians! Children! Mostly on *one* side!

ASAF. All true, and yet the Palestinian population keeps *growing*, so –

BARON. There's more than one way to commit a genocide.

ASAF. There's not, actually, there's *one*, and it's by killing people so quickly that, if it keeps *up*, they'll be *gone*. Sorry, is *that* controversial now? Is there a new kind of genocide where the target population *doubles*?

FARID. *(To* **RACHEL** *–)* This... I can't –

ASAF. No, it's tragic. But there are fewer Jews in the world right now, today, than there were in 1938. That's a fucking genocide.

RACHEL. *(To* **FARID** *–)* Hey, hey, it's okay. We don't need him. We don't even need him involved. Now we've started we can go on without him or find someone else. I'm sorry, okay? You were right when we met him.

ASAF. What? About what.

RACHEL. Nothing.

ASAF. No, what did he say? *(To* **FARID** *–)* What'd you say?

RACHEL. That you wouldn't really *help* us.

ASAF. *(To* **FARID** *–)* Is that right.

FARID. Yes.

ASAF. And you knew as soon as you met me. Interesting.

FARID. Yes because I *have* met you. Not you *specifically*, but *you*: the sympathetic ear. So interested. So *brave*. I used to be grateful! Someone willing to entertain my suffering! And then each time I'd watch as, bit by bit, well: *this*. After the listening come the questions. Then defensiveness, then anger, and pretty soon here we are at: "Don't complain until we kill you *faster*." And so, yes, forgive me if, fool me once, fool me ten times, by now I'm not so grateful for this slower path to the same destination, where, in the end, you side with your people and I with mine.

RACHEL. *(She doesn't love this last idea –)* Well –

FARID. *(Acknowledging* **RACHEL**, *but still to* **ASAF** *–)* Yes but the problem for you now is that there is a new generation. Not just here but there. Here it's those who will no longer accept at face value the propaganda that has obtained for so long. But *there*? There you have the *real* problem which is a new generation with little-to-no faith in non-violence.

ASAF. Um –

FARID. Yes: "When did Palestinians try non-violence?" Constantly! Again and again! The First Intifada was non-violent in 1987! It was demonstrations, strikes. The Second, yes, had the bus bombings, which were, to coin a phrase, the aggressive policy of a single faction, but the rest was, again, marches, protests – but, you see, this is what I don't have *time* for any longer! To *educate* you! I am so *tired*! You think Isaac Roth's bold assertion that *perhaps* Israel harbored territorial ambitions early on is some kind of revolutionary *conclusion*? It's the *starting* place! It's *kindergarten*! There is a whole parallel *history* you've *chosen* not to learn! You know nothing of our culture, its beauty, variety, depth. What spurs radicalization. Who benefits. "Where is the Palestinian Gandhi?" they cry. "If they could only follow a leader like that!" But there have been dozens. Hundreds. We have them now! Have you heard of Issa Amro? Jawad Siam? Nasser Nawaj'ah? Peaceful activists, all. Routinely beaten, arrested, detained for protesting the theft or bulldozing of their own homes or for no cause at all! The Tamimi family of Nabi Saleh has for *ten years* tried once a week to *peacefully walk* to the natural spring *stolen* from their village by settlers. They are fired upon with live ammunition. People have been killed. The family's own cousin by a *tear gas* canister shot point blank into his face. *(Off* **ASAF** *–)* Yes, I know, terrible, you oppose it, fervently, so fervently! You condemn *each individual indefensible act*! Yet you will not condemn as indefensible the national entity that carries them out! "Well because *most* soldiers surely don't *behave* this way" – you see, by now I can do it on my own! – "not *Israel's* soldiers." They do, though. "Well, *if* they do, they must be the *exceptions*." No. It is the *policy*. "Well then there must be a *reason*. What did *you* do to *provoke* them?"

BARON. Yeah.

FARID. *(To* **BARON** *–)* Yes. *You* know. And *this* is how it is the same. *(Back to* **ASAF** *–)* Not on some mathematical level of analogic perfection. But in the *experience* of moving through the world as the threat of violence incarnate. They don't need to see the bomb, the gun. We *are* the bomb. We *are* the gun. I can feel it happening in this room now, because of my anger! "Look at the angry Arab! Just as we thought!" Well yes, *now* I am. After *years* of being quiet and humble and peaceful, only to learn it makes no difference! That, in fact, it makes them *angrier* because, if I am peaceful, then who is the monster? It makes them hate themselves and so beat us harder for seventy-five years!!! *(Beat.)* That is what I left family behind in, my *mother*, to be *here*, and come to this temple of ideas, and speak, so I will speak: Palestine must be free. Fuck the *status quo* and anyone who supports it. Fuck Hamas! Who have not held elections since 2006 and are by now codependent with the Israeli government, who could topple them if they chose, but *fund* them instead because they prefer their tunnels and rockets to anything else that might emerge from Gaza. Fuck the Palestinian Authority, who are by now simply a security arm of the IDF in the West Bank, where settlers burn homes and fields now with impunity. And the other Arab leaders, for that matter, who use us to turn the anger of their people away from their own autocracies. There is no justification for the subjugation of my people. Even though, you're right, a perfect democracy would not flower there overnight, correct. Even though, yes, more would die. Your people. My people. I do not *wish* it, I would *condemn* it, *fervently*, but there would be attacks, and some would succeed. But this will happen anyway. If nothing changes, it's *all* that will happen, all that *can*. Which is why *I* have come to think that it must be the *alternative* that our enemies fear most: that finally, after all this time, if given a chance to thrive...we *would*. *(To* **BARON** *–)* Call me, brother. We'll talk.

BARON. Yeah.

> *(***FARID** *bumps fists with* **BARON** *and exits. A moment. Then –)*

RACHEL. It's not just about numbers. It's about a language of erasure. Telling a whole people they don't exist, just cuz it would be more convenient for you if they didn't. *That's* what you can't unsee once you see it. And I lost family in the *Shoah*, too, Professor, which is why *my* mother told me I'm breaking her heart. But then I just remember what it's all cost *him*, and I think: fuck it, this is *right*. *(Beat.)* Anyway, so: I think we'll be seeking a new adviser for J-FIT. One more aligned with our core values. Turns out you *are* Jewish. You're just not that progressive, cool, or *young*. *(To the* **OTHERS** *–)* See you at the march.

> *(***RACHEL** *exits. A moment. Then –)*

NAKIA. *(Lifting the document –)* But other than that it's fine?

ASAF. Look –

BARON. What's happening to Black folks in this country is a slow-motion genocide.

> *(Beat.)*

ASAF. *(Simply –)* Okay.

BARON. Okay?

ASAF. I don't care what you call it. I want to stand with you. *(Then, indicating after **FARID** –)* And him too. *(Long pause.)* And so please understand I'm not saying that anything is more urgent than that right now. Than you. *(To **NAKIA** –)* Maybe all I'm asking is why this… *(The document.)* …Call to protect persecuted people… leaves one persecuted people out? Why doesn't this say anything about protecting Jews?

    (Beat.)

NAKIA. Huh. *(Beat.) Is* there an answer that would satisfy? Or is the real problem here that any criticism of Jews, by *Black* people, is off limits?

ASAF. I didn't say that.

NAKIA. Yeah. But –

BARON. Why?

NAKIA. *(To **ASAF** –)* Should you do the honors or should I? *(A beat. Then, to **BARON** –)* See, Asaf here is from Berkeley which is, y'know, *next* to Oakland. So he grew up hearing stories from old hippies about the early Civil Rights movement, in which Jews did play a role, and so what is at least partly bothering him is *our* failure to, as a result, forever prostrate ourselves and remain grateful.

ASAF. I didn't say *any* of that. *(A beat. Then –)* Though, since you bring it up, we did cofound the NAACP.

NAKIA. Yup. *This* old song.

ASAF. *(Continuous –)* Two-*thirds* of Freedom Riders were Jewish. The lawyers in Loving. Scottsboro. Should I go on?

NAKIA. Two-thirds of *white* Freedom Riders were Jewish, Asaf. You're leaving out the Freedom Riders who were *Black*.

ASAF. And so, yeah, there *is* something a bit galling about the lack of solidarity. Let alone the weird strain of antisemitism that runs from Farrakhan to Kanye West, that bullshit about how *we* ran the *slave* trade, or brought back the *Klan* –

NAKIA. *(To* **BARON** *–) And* he's leaving out that, after '64? And *just* as the redlining that kept us *both* out the white neighborhood got lifted on *them* but not on us, they joined all the other good white liberals in declaring the struggle over, and then moved out. *(To* **ASAF** *–)* Though some of y'all *did* hold onto the buildings and hike up the rent.

ASAF. *(Urgently, to* **BARON** *–) That* was not representative.

NAKIA. Oh and Kanye *is*?

BARON. *(Trying to break in –)* Yeah. Hey –

NAKIA. But what *I* find galling is this whole notion of a *quid pro quo*. That fighting Jim Crow, and segregation, and *lynching* wasn't a moral imperative –

ASAF. It *was*. Of *course* it was.

NAKIA. – But rather just a kind of *down* payment on Black *loyalty*.

ASAF. *That* is *offensive*.

NAKIA. This young man's cousin was *murdered*.

ASAF. I *know* that.

NAKIA. Well if you *know* then what the fuck are we *talking* about, Asaf!? Let me ask *you* something. *Do* you love Black people? Or is our pain just a way for you to burnish your liberal *bona fides* while actually changing *nothing*?

ASAF. How can you *ask* me that!? How can you still fucking ask me that?! We fight for *everyone*! We *always* have! We just *also need* to protect *ourselves*! What's it gonna take for you to fucking *believe us*?!

BARON. *(Loudly enough to finally draw focus –)* Yeah,
um...! *(Then –)* So I'm starting to get the feeling that
the two of you maybe have some shit to work out
between you? So I'm gonna go. *(To* **ASAF** *–)* But first:
I don't have a problem with Jewish people. I mean, I
didn't really *know* any growing up? Or maybe I did and
just thought they were...other white people. Either way,
I really never gave it much thought. *(Beat.)* And then I
got in here. And the challenge, after *literally* growing
up in the shadow of this place? Was to see if I could
be *in* it but not *of* it. And then it was exactly what I
thought, I mean all that shit in my screenplay was *true*:
getting stopped going into my own dorm, or professors
who act skeptical 'til you turn something in but then if
it's *too good* they're *suspicious*, or the dining hall having
stained glass pictures of slaves while ninety percent of
the other Black people you see are the ones *working*
there. But you don't talk about it. Cuz you *know* no
one wants to hear it. So the whole time you're just like,
"That's fine. That's why I'm *here*. To be in a position to
change the narrative later on." And then I took your
class. And I didn't come in being like: "*This* is the story
I'm gonna tell." I was still thinking no one wants to hear
that. *You* were the one who was like, "But what's *your*
story. Maybe start there." I mean, probably you say
that to everyone, but it *meant* something. *(Beat.)* And,
like I said, I doubt you're the first Jewish person I ever
met, but you're the *first one* who I *thought* about how
he was Jewish, and what *that* might mean. That that
might be *why* you could be like: "Naw, *fuck* this place."
Cuz you were *also in* it but not *of* it. That and the fact
that you barely really work here. *(Pause.)* So when this
shit happened to Deronte, and I had to go to people,
to ask for help? I was least worried to come to you. It
was easiest to come to you. So I've been listening. And
I think I get why it's complicated. But what I still don't
understand is how, after watching that video... *(Then,
off* **ASAF** *–)* You did watch it, right?

ASAF. I didn't *have* to. I took your *word*.

BARON. Apparently *not* though. *(Beat.)* Huh. Yeah, okay. *(A beat. Then –)* Yeah. Um. So, okay: if your problem is you feel like you have to choose? Maybe look at it like you *get* to choose. Cuz I don't know if the chances of some Jews dying somewhere, someday go up if you're standing by my side? But I *do* know the chances of *me* dying, right now, today, go way, way up if you're not. *(Beat.)* I'll let you know if I finish that screenplay though. I've got an idea now for what could happen in the end.

ASAF. Baron –

BARON. *(To **NAKIA** –)* I'll see you.

> *(**BARON** exits. Then –)*

NAKIA. *(Pause.)* This is about the shrimp, isn't it.

ASAF. What? No.

NAKIA. It is. It's about those goddamn shrimp. But you know what? *That* is what shrimp *look* like.

ASAF. Fine! But you didn't have to be so mean about it!

NAKIA. And *you* didn't have to be so sensitive!

ASAF. Fine!

NAKIA. Fine!

> *(Pause.)*

ASAF. Except I wasn't just being sensitive about shrimp, was I.

NAKIA. No?

ASAF. No. Something else had happened that day. Do you remember? Why would you. *I* didn't, 'til a little bit ago. We'd been with some of your friends, your super-militant activist friends, who always... I mean they were nice, but they were always also laughing at me too, a little, like: "Oh, poor innocent Asaf, so much to learn."

NAKIA. And that upset you?

ASAF. No, it was not unkind, it was fine, but this time, one of them, your, uh, friend Tariq actually, he... We were talking about 9/11. The intelligence failure, how Bush ignored the warnings, and we *were* getting a little conspiracy-ish: "Did they let it happen so they could have their wars." But then Tariq goes: "And why is no one even looking *into* the fact that there were no Jews in the towers that day?" *(Beat.)* And I was like, um, I personally *know* people who had friends and relatives who died in those towers who were Jewish, and he sorta backed up, but sorta *not*, like, "I'm not saying *all* Jews, but you should really read up on it," and everyone was sorta uncomfortable and then we moved on, and I *let* us, cuz... Well cuz I was in *love* with you, and also I just didn't want to cause a *problem*, but later, at dinner, you snapped at me about the stupid shrimp, and I think what I was really thinking was: "I guess attacks on me don't count."

NAKIA. And you think *I* didn't have those moments? With your *mom*? "She has such strong opinions!"

ASAF. My mother *loved* you.

NAKIA. Or your friends, your old roommate, joined a hedge fund? "Isn't the *real* problem making everything about race? I'm just asking."

ASAF. He wasn't a *friend*, he was an *old roommate*, and I said *immediately* after, "I'm *sorry*. That guy's an *asshole*." And what I *didn't* do was start *sleeping* with him the second we broke *up*.

NAKIA. Is *that* what this is about?

ASAF. I mean, it wouldn't hurt to put "hating Jews" higher on your list of *deal*-breakers, but no, what it's *about* is that *this* time I'm not going to stay quiet so I can sit at the progressive cool table when I *know* something is wrong.

NAKIA. *(The document –) This* doesn't say Jews planned 9/11.

ASAF. No it doesn't say anything *about* us except as *oppressors*. Look: we can handle anger at some slumlords. *I* don't even mind if old school Christ-killer shit crops up at Black church sometimes. But it's when we hear tropes about how we *control* everything that our alarm bells go off, so when a document about the nexus of forces that rule the globe makes *special mention* –

NAKIA. Dear God, for the hundredth time –

ASAF. When what the French did in Mali creates a genuine threat that the French might have to leave *France*, *then* tell me it's the same.

NAKIA. Come on.

ASAF. No, I get the *argument* now: you want to end Jewish supremacy in the one place it's ever kind of actually existed. Say we did it! Fine, *I* don't support ethnostates, not at the cost of democracy. But what *actually happens next* to those Jews? And why can't we even *acknowledge* the *existence* of hostility towards them *for* being Jews? And could it be because you *sense* it would make it harder to galvanize your movement, cuz it's maybe not ending "supremacy" that's getting everyone so fired up so much as ending the *presence* of *Jews*?

NAKIA. *Fuck* you.

ASAF. I'm just asking.

NAKIA. If antisemitism *fuels* social *justice*? No. People sure like to use bullshit *accusations* of it to shut us *down*, though. Though, despite what an *asshole* you can be, I did *not* expect it from *you*. No, *you* fuckin' hang on now. You're gonna come at the *left*? When the *right* – who don't give a shit about you, *or* Israel, so much as they just love oil, selling weapons, and killing Arabs – have a *political base* of *actual* torch-waving mobs chanting "Jews will not *replace* us"? How *dare* you suggest they aren't the real threat?

ASAF. Yeah, no, good point, like: what about *them*, you're saying?

NAKIA. *Yes!*

ASAF. Cuz, like...what about *them*?

NAKIA. What? Oh –

ASAF. Uh-huh.

NAKIA. *That's* not... No.

ASAF. You don't understand. I'm not saying they aren't the threat. Of *course* white nationalist Christian fascism is the big threat! Do you see me bothering to argue with *them*? I'm not *delusional*. What I'm *saying* is, to *beat* them, we need a left with *moral credibility*, and one that for *whatever reason* can't fight antisemitism –

NAKIA. Who says we can't?! It's just not a part of the *system* we're *currently* trying to *dismantle*!

ASAF. But that's *wrong*! Nakia, that's a mistake! Those guys, chanting? What do you think they *mean*? They can't stand the idea that Black and brown people could create or beat them at *anything*, so they've convinced themselves antiracism and immigration reform and even *hip*-hop are all part of a plot to replace the white race, puppeteered by *Jews* who, by the way? *They* don't think are *white*. *(Pointing to himself –) Even the white ones!* Antisemitism is not some *separate thing* off to the side of capitalism, colonialism, patriarchy, and white supremacy; it's a *justification* for them. You *have* to fight it.

NAKIA. With what copious fucking *resources*, Asaf!? *Yeah* I'm worried about folks dying *today*! State violence and ethnic cleansing *today*! I can't spend time *also fighting* some Nazi-cracker delusion!

ASAF. *All* hate is a delusion! I'm just saying why aren't we entitled to the same protections as you?

NAKIA. You are! You just don't *need* them right *now*!

ASAF. *The idea that we don't need them is what we need protection from!* You write so passionately about so many things, just write this, too: that Jews are at risk for being Jews, that it takes the *form* of saying we're *powerful*, and so for *anyone* to say we *can't* be at risk *because* we're powerful is the lie that kills us! What terrible thing do you think will happen if you *say* that, just that, in there? What are you afraid of?

NAKIA. I am not afraid.

ASAF. Then why. Cuz you don't beat Sauron by wearing the ring; you have to throw it in the fucking volcano. *(Beat.)* That's from –

NAKIA. I know. You made me go to all of those *with* you. *(Pause.)* Look, I'm sorry if this is painful for you, Asaf. I mean, I can see that it is. And I'd never say Jews aren't at risk – they face persecution, like so many do. But I do not, to coin a phrase, believe that these two struggles are actually the same struggle. And I will not be distracted from the work. *That's* why.

ASAF. Okay. *(Beat.)* Okay, yeah, in that case, due to concerns I should maybe have raised earlier, I can't sign your manifesto after all. Please remove my name.

NAKIA. Do you know why things couldn't work out between us, Asaf?

> *(He has turned to go, but now stops –)*

ASAF. That's... *(Beat.)* Why?

NAKIA. Because for all your intelligence, and eloquence, and even sympathy, when it really costs you something, you can't put anybody else's pain before your own.

> *(**ASAF** and **GWEN**. She stares at him. Then –)*

ASAF. What.

GWEN. What do you mean "what"? It's all over campus.

ASAF. What?

GWEN. You, *shouting* at students, getting fired from that *group*, insulting Black people and Arabs?

ASAF. *Whoa.* What? It's, no, it was not like that.

GWEN. Oh? What was it like?

ASAF. It was a *very* complicated, five-sided conversation. In which I was *repeatedly* provoked.

GWEN. I don't care if everybody held up copies of *Mein Kampf* and goose-stepped up your fucking *asshole*, Asaf! I *told* you it was delicate!

ASAF. I know! I was just trying to –!

GWEN. What? What were you trying to do?

ASAF. I...! *(Beat.)* You told me to join an activity! *(Off* **GWEN** *–)* No, sorry, look: that's...horrifying. And I can see why it makes things harder for you and I want to fix it. I will fix it. *(Beat.)* How do I fix it?

GWEN. Isn't it obvious?

ASAF. Is it?

GWEN. The Grand Jury in the Deronte Lee case is about to announce if they're indicting those cops.

ASAF. Oh, okay. I mean *good*.

GWEN. Well not necessarily but, one way or another, there's gonna be a march and, when that happens, you should come with me.

ASAF. Really.

GWEN. Yes. You're *lucky*, actually. To have an opportunity to throw support behind everyone you just offended so soon.

ASAF. Um, okay, but won't that be...?

GWEN. What.

ASAF. Kind of *transparent*? That I'd be doing it just to...?

GWEN. Um: *yeah*, Asaf, it is *less than ideal*. It is certainly preferable to do things for the right *reasons*. Not just the right *thing* but with the exact right fucking *impetus* behind it, what a joyful way to go through life, except I literally don't know anyone who gets to do it. I *definitely* don't know anybody who *expects* it.

ASAF. Right, and: just so I understand: it's also good for *you* if I go because it will help smooth over the university expansion.

GWEN. That is *one* effect it *may* have if you're *lucky*.

ASAF. Yeah but that's the one that interests *you* the most.

GWEN. It's my job.

ASAF. Even though, *really*, all you're doing is helping what's essentially a real-estate venture seize more undervalued land from poor people. No no, I know, there'll be tutoring, *amazing*, and for a year or two you'll protect local business until Target or Subway or whoever make offers just *so good* that what were you supposed to do? And for that *I'm* s'posed to grovel? So *you* can erase another Bottomville?

GWEN. Your friend Nakia tell you that story? *(Off* **ASAF** *–)* And, lemme guess: the school and city colluded to make the neighborhood worse on purpose 'til a student got stabbed so they'd have an excuse to destroy it and rebuild.

ASAF. Is that not what happened?

GWEN. No, it happened. Question though: who got stabbed? *(Beat.)* Come on, who was he? Why was he *living* out there? You're so interested in local history now. There's a campus, there's *dorms*, why was a kid from the University renting an apartment in Bottomville in 1960? Care to guess? No one ever tells this part. *(Beat.)* He was a Chinese exchange student. He was living there because he wasn't welcome on campus. Meanwhile, *off* campus, he's such a symbol of the university he gets knifed to death. But things have changed, right? Except that the next time they needed an ambassador to a Black neighborhood they hired me: palatable to all; trusted by none.

ASAF. Okay. So fuck *them*.

GWEN. *No*, Asaf, *not* fuck them, because if I say "fuck them" they will just replace me with someone who *actually* doesn't give a shit, and that neighborhood *will* be gone, just *gone*. Whereas, if *I* have this job, I can at least *try* to Trojan Horse this into something *good*. Look, I understand what it's like to be part of a minority regarded with fear and suspicion cuz of our success. Not to mention having a homeland with a somewhat dangerous regime on its Northern border. But, even if I didn't, Asaf, I would *try* because that's what *marriage* is. That's what *loving* someone is. It's seeing the other person, and compromising, and helping them, and right now I need for my goddamn husband to fucking *help me*.

> (**ASAF** *and* **THE RABBI. THE RABBI** *is played by the actor who plays* **NAKIA.**)

ASAF. Rabbi?

RABBI. Yes?

ASAF. *(Seeing her –)* Oh. *(Beat.)* Hi.

RABBI. Not quite what you were expecting. Yeah, I get that a lot. Although, you know the old joke, right?

ASAF. Uh, which one?

RABBI. Jewish man from Brooklyn goes to Shanghai? *(Then, off his blank look –)* And it's beautiful. But also intense, overwhelming and he feels out of place and so he asks the guy at the hotel if there's a synagogue nearby and, to his surprise, there is. So he goes, and it's Saturday morning service, but everyone's Chinese: the Rabbi's Chinese, and they do the service in Hebrew and Chinese, but it's familiar enough that it makes him feel more at home. But, through it all, the congregants keep throwing glances his way, and then at the end a bunch of them crowd around and say, like: "What are you doing here?" And the man says, "Well, I'm staying nearby," and they say, "No no: what are you doing at a *synagogue*?" And he's like, "Oh! Well, I'm Jewish." And they say, "Funny. You don't look Jewish."

ASAF. Heheheh. *(Beat.)* I did know that one actually.

RABBI. It's a good one, right?

ASAF. Yeah.

> *(Pause.)*

RABBI. So what can I do for you?

ASAF. Right, sorry. My name's Asaf Sternheim? And –

RABBI. I know who you are.

ASAF. Oh! *(Then, realizing why –)* Oh. So: maybe you also know why I'm here.

RABBI. I have an inkling. Cutting it a little close, aren't you?

ASAF. What?

RABBI. Aren't they about to start the march right now?

ASAF. Yeah but the verdict might not come down for another couple hours, so –

RABBI. Still doesn't seem like enough time to cover something like this.

ASAF. *(Deadpan –)* Tell me about it. *(Beat.)* But, yeah, I'll get right to the point.

RABBI. Okay.

ASAF. Okay. *(Beat.)* Because I'm not someone who would have ever said my life has been in any way shaped by antisemitism. I grew up in an area with a big Jewish community where I joined a youth group. I went to a liberal arts college full of Jews. And then I moved to New York City. I can count on one hand the number of times something actually antisemitic has been said in my presence and have fingers left over. *(Beat.)* But it's also shaped *everything.* My mother's mother was Polish. Her family had to leave for Palestine in the '20s because of pogroms. My mother's father was sent from Vienna to a Kibbutz as a teenager with the rest of his family meant to follow but they didn't leave in time. My mother's parents divorced when she was young and her stepfather was an Iraqi Jew whose family left Bazra when they didn't love their prospects there. My father's family was German. At least 'til they were told, rather emphatically, that they weren't. I never think about any of this. I never write about it. But it's literally why I exist. It's why *any* of my grandparents were alive to meet so my parents could be born. Israel is why I exist. *(Beat.)* Which isn't to say it's therefore off the hook for everything, forever, on the *contrary*, it means I have to be *extra on guard* against my own tribalism, and that's why it's been so troubling, over the course of this, to have heard myself arguing points of view, the *equivalent* of which, on any other issue, I would find, honestly, repellent. *(Beat.)* But the left is a tribe too, of which I'm also a member, and what are the chances *we're* right about everything *else*? Everything *easy* for me to believe cuz, up to now, it's cost me nothing? Maybe everything we think we think is just the sum of all our loyalties to all the tribes to which we variously belong and it's *only* where two of those are in conflict that we can even *begin* to see things clearly. *(Beat.)* Except one's deeper. That's the other thing I've learned. *One* is...every value and position I've held my entire adult life, sure, but the *other* is thousands of years old and in my DNA and it is *warning* me. In a way I've never felt before. Which, lucky me, right? What a blessed existence, not to have lived in daily terror, so shut up and take it, except... I *am* afraid. *(A beat. Then, simply admitting –)* I'm afraid. *(Beat.)* And I don't know whether to dismiss the fear as irrational *because* it's so instinctive or, for that same reason, treat it as wisdom. Because when the *myth* about you is that, no matter how few of you there are, you're in control...*defending* yourself can only ever prove it true. And the only way to *disprove* it is: allow yourself to be destroyed and we *tried* that once already. And all we got was people saying it never happened. Actually, that's not all. We also got a country. That now defends itself in ways *I* find increasingly difficult to defend. I'm afraid of how they hate us. And of our fear turning us into the very thing they hate.

> *(Beat.)*

RABBI. Sorry, *what's* the question?

ASAF. The question is what do I *do*?

RABBI. Ah.

ASAF. In this situation.

RABBI. I can't tell you what to do.

ASAF. Okay, well: what ought a hypothetical Jew to do?

RABBI. I can't tell you what a hypothetical Jew should do either.

ASAF. Isn't that what rabbis are for?

RABBI. *(Shrugging –)* Eh.

ASAF. Great. *(Beat.)* Okay how 'bout this: in the Talmud it says: "He or she who can protest but does not is accomplice in the act."

RABBI. Very good.

ASAF. Yeah but *which* protest? And which act, or, what about when protesting one act you want to protest involves *another* act that you also want to protest? Is there another quote that can help me best make use of that first quote?

RABBI. Well... Hillel the Elder said: "Im ein ani li, mi li? U–"

ASAF. *(Overlapping, taking over, singing to a little melody.)* "Uchsheani la'atzmi ma ani? Ve im lo achshav eh matai? Eh matai?"

RABBI. You know it.

ASAF. We...sang it in my youth group. Remind me what it means?

RABBI. "If I am not for myself, who will be for me? If I am *only* for myself, what am I? And if not now, when?"

　　　(Beat.)

ASAF. Well that's no help at *all*!

RABBI. Professor Sternheim, I just met you? But I'm gonna go out on a limb and say that the thing *you* need may not be more *words*.

　　　*(**ASAF** opens his mouth to respond. Then does not. Then –)*

Anyway, I should get there *myself*, so –

ASAF. What? Oh, right. So: *you're* going.

RABBI. Well, I mean: did you see the video?

ASAF. No, I... I mean I *believe* what everyone has said. I just didn't actually *watch*.

RABBI. Oh. *(Beat.)* I mean, that's fine, there's...different schools of thought about the *ethics* of that kind of thing. Though maybe that's not *why* you didn't. *(Then –)* Look, there *are* other quotes, bits of wisdom.

They're part of what drew *me*, which is a whole other story. But there's something else. Beyond the ideas or...beneath them. See, *ideas* don't *feel*. That's why they're appealing. We can stay in our heads forever, turning them, following them to infinity, and be safe because, in your head, you can't be hurt. Whereas bodies can. And so – and all traumatized people do this, not just Jews – we build a wall between our bodies and our minds. But Judaism also wants you to remember you have a body. The Hasids, the Hasidic mystics, have a practice: "Yerida l'tzorekh aliyah." "Descending to ascend." Basically, you sit down. Close your eyes. And...*feel*. First, your body. Head to toe. Then every emotion. Fear. Hate. Despair. Hope. Love. And then...what's beyond.

ASAF. Which is what?

RABBI. If you believe the mystics? God.

ASAF. I'm an atheist.

RABBI. Then whatever comes. *(Beat.)* The other thing is you have to be alone. Stay as long as you like.

> *(The* **RABBI** *exits.* **ASAF** *is alone. A moment. He looks at a nearby chair. There it is: empty. Waiting. But he doesn't want to approach it. He walks slowly along one edge of the room, keeping the chair in view, but not, as yet, getting any closer. Then he stops and regards it, again. Then, warily, he approaches and sits. He's not sure what to do with his hands – do they go in his lap? To his sides? Doesn't matter. He puts them in his lap. She said to close his eyes, too, but this step feels scary as well, so he doesn't do it, yet. During this, gradually, from outside, chanting becomes audible – the protest is underway. Then, as* **ASAF** *continues to sit, and to not yet close*

*his eyes, the sounds get louder, filling the
room, echoing, ghostly, louder, and louder,
the lights getting brighter as well, perhaps
illuminating the audience itself, until, at the
peak of this...)*

(**ASAF** *closes his eyes. Blackout.*)

End of Play